Hands
on the Wheel

A
Sinfully Erotic
Trucker Romance

by

Margaret Harlowe

HANDS ON THE WHEEL:

A SINFULLY EROTIC TRUCKER ROMANCE

ISBN-10: 1523694068

ISBN-13: 978-1523694068

For those who are
strong enough
to be gentle.

CHAPTER 1

SARA

The metallic purple cab sparkled in the glaring sun as the semi rolled into the grill's large parking lot. Sara Cooke read the fancy lettering on the driver's door: "Hank Werner Trucking, Cheyenne, Wyoming."

She'd never seen this rig before.

She set the coffee pot down and watched the driver climb out. A cowboy trucker. They were a dime a dozen in Wyoming. As he sauntered across the asphalt, he glanced back at the massive eighteen-wheeler and pulled his worn straw cowboy hat lower on his forehead.

Inside the grill, he headed to a window booth in her station. He left his hat on. That was typical of these cowboy types. Tall and lanky, he wore polished black cowboy boots – the kind with square toes and nice stitching. His Wrangler jeans fit him just right. He even had one of those oval silver belt buckles. Probably a rodeo trophy. Most of those were. The long sleeves of his dark red western shirt were rolled up, revealing a blue tattoo on his left arm.

"Howdy," she said, setting water and a menu in front of him.

"Hey there." He glanced up with a friendly smile and opened the plastic-covered menu.

A long salt-and-pepper ponytail streamed down his back. Not many cowboy truckers in these parts sported long hair. Or tattoos,

1

for that matter. Still, he dressed like a good old-fashioned cowboy trucker, not like the young, sloppy ones. This guy seemed like the real deal, his sideburns and mustache bright white against his tanned face. "I'll give you a minute," she told him.

He nodded. "Restroom?"

Sara pointed it out. As he ambled down the hall she swallowed hard. He looked good in his Wranglers. The jeans cupped his muscular ass in a decidedly sexy way. She shook it off, cursing herself. Of course this guy would already be taken. Men like him were always too good to be true. Sara felt her face heat up, embarrassed by the pull she felt in her groin. She hadn't felt that pull for a long time.

How ridiculous, she thought, suddenly as shy and insecure as a school girl. She picked up an order, tossing her head. Here she was, forty-three and divorced, for crying out loud. Since the cancer she'd been celibate. Maybe it was getting to her. Her scar wasn't that bad, but that damned Johnny had made her feel untouchable.

Sara shrugged. She was feeling pretty good these days – good enough to work double shifts often, to help Annie and the others. She liked helping and she needed the money, especially now that Lexie was talking about going to college. Sara knew her ex, Lexie's dad, wouldn't be good for any support whatsoever.

The late morning sun beamed through the grill's tall windows. It was too early for lunch for most folks. Annie would be here soon. Sara busied herself filling up the glass sugar containers.

Of course she felt untouchable. Her cheeks flamed hotter as she recalled the horrified look on Johnny's face that night. Sara wished she could forget it. The one guy she'd let in. Just her luck! That was six months after the surgery. She'd never thought he would act like such an ass, pulling back when he felt and saw the radiation scar on her left breast. He'd given her a quick excuse and left.

She hadn't heard from him since.

Thank God he never came into the Flying Bison Grill any more.

2

What a dim-wit. On the other hand, it might be nice if he came in one more time, so she could toss scalding coffee in his face.

Sara knew it was his loss. But why did she have this feeling of shame?

She tossed her hair again. She'd always been attractive. Even beautiful, some would say. Now she felt deformed, thanks to Johnny.

She should go see a shrink or something. It was time for a change. A big one. Sara was tired of watching these truckers come and go. For the longest time she'd wanted to join them on the road.

She glanced out the window as another rig pulled in. Maybe one of these guys would teach her how to drive his semi. The thing was, Sara couldn't afford to take any time off. This waitressing job paid the bills. More or less. The Flying Bison was the best place to eat in Chugwater, and the tips were good. It was part of the Flying Bison Inn, the only lodging in this one-horse town. The grill wasn't actually a truck stop, but the truckers liked the food.

As Mr. Sexy Wranglers passed behind her, she caught the scent of Aramis. Her favorite. Sara kept her eyes on the sugar container in front of her. Just a faint scent. Perfect. She hated most men's colognes. But she loved this one. She inhaled the wood and leather aroma.

She waited until he was seated, then walked over. "Ready to order?"

"You betcha. Taco salad with ranch, and black coffee."

"Got it." Sara put her pencil back behind her ear and looked into his suntanned face. When he grinned, his sloping hazel eyes seemed kind. He was handsome in that cowboy hat. His appraising gaze took her breath away.

Don't be ridiculous, she told herself again.

When she brought his coffee, he grinned again. "How did Chugwater get its name?" he asked.

"You must be a newbie."

"Yep. Just moved to Cheyenne."

"Chugwater was named after the sound of bison hitting the creek at the bottom of the cliff."

"Seriously?"

"Yep. Long ago the Mandan hunted buffalo by driving them over the cliffs here. When the animals landed, they made a chug sound. They called it 'water at the place where the buffalo chug' because of the stream."

The pick-up bell rang.

"SARA!" the cook hollered.

***

His name was Hank. As he left Sara noticed his graceful, athletic stride. It was a relaxed gait, not a swagger. He struck her as quietly confident – a guy with nothing to prove.

She enjoyed men like that.

Sara watched the shiny purple rig roll into the street, its twin chrome stacks flashing in the sun. She smiled to herself. She'd caught him checking out her ass as she leaned over the counter. She knew her ass looked good, even in this stupid waitress uniform. If only she could wear something else to work. It would be fun to show off her clothes. And the new strappy high heels she'd just bought.

She was pretty sure Hank would be back soon, and not just because he liked the food. She smoothed her hair back, smiling to herself again.

Sara heard someone come in. Glancing up, her heart sank.

Her ex-husband's angry eyes stared back at her.

What the holy Hell was Richard doing here?

CHAPTER 2

HANK

The waitress refilled his coffee and blushed a furious shade of pink that matched her waitress outfit. "Sara," her name tag said. Maybe she was shy. Sweet. He loved that pink uniform and the darker pink apron over it.

"Dessert?" Her voice was husky.

"What's good?" He looked into her soft gray eyes. There was a vague sadness there.

"Homemade strawberry-rhubarb pie."

"Lay it on me."

"OK." She scribbled on her pad. "Anything on it?"

"The works."

"You got it." Sara darted around, filling coffee cups and taking orders. Her shiny, gold-streaked hair curled into her jawline, the sides pulled up and pinned in a way that accented her sharp cheekbones. She wore white gym shoes that seemed designed for racing around the restaurant. She kept reading glasses tucked into her uniform blouse and a pencil behind her ear. Sara struck him as a no-nonsense woman. But not a hardened one.

He watched her lean over the window to pick up an order, her uniform skirt hugging her tight little ass. Hank's cock sprang to life, pressing insistently against his jeans. That little curve below her ass turned him on. So did the backs of her shapely legs, and the honey color of her skin. Hank imagined walking over there right now and taking her from behind. Just like that.

If only things could be that simple.

He would run his hands up the outsides of those caramel legs and up her sweet hips, pushing her skirt up until it was bunched around her narrow waist. He would hold her against him, kiss her neck, and explore her with his hands. When he knew she wanted him, he would bend her over and give her a good, hard fucking. She looked like she was made for it.

Hank didn't mind admitting he was an ass man. Always had been. It was just who he was. Done right, fucking from behind could be just as tender and loving as any other position. He knew how to do it right – the places to touch, and when, and how. From behind was ten times more exciting than any other way.

He wondered if she liked it like that. Many women didn't. Many of them felt it was animalistic, and required them to give up too much control. But some loved it. Dear God, let her be one of those! He wanted her so bad, his mouth had gone dry.

She was perfect. Sara had the finest ass he'd seen for… How long had it been? Hank hadn't been hot like this for anyone since Becky. The thought of his late wife made his stomach clench.

He couldn't think about her. Losing her to cancer still hurt too much. Hank rubbed his neck and sipped his coffee, keeping his nose over the cup to inhale the steam. During the three years since Becky's death, he hadn't been attracted enough to a woman to do anything about it. This one, though, this Sara, was already turning his crank.

She set his pie in front of him. "Enjoy."

"Thanks." He caught her scent. What was it? Something familiar and subtle. Maybe bath powder. Or lotion. Her face was flushed pink again. Was she noticing him, too? Just think how pink her face would be if she knew what he'd just been imagining doing to her. He liked her shyness. It made him even hotter. Sara probably had no idea how sexy and pretty she was.

He had to have her.

He shook himself and shifted so that his cock wasn't pressing so hard against his jeans. He attacked his pie, his eyes on his plate. He was probably too old for her. Here he was in his fifties and she was probably only in her thirties, for crying out loud.

He hated his receding hairline. Some women were turned off by that. The pretty waitress hadn't seen his balding head yet. Hank had gotten in the habit of leaving his hat on in cafes. It was accepted here in Wyoming. Especially cowboy hats, of course. They were sacred. He reached under the brim and scratched his forehead, which had broken out in a sweat.

He washed a piece of pie down with coffee. Why the hell was he worrying over things he could do nothing about? You'd think he'd be used to his balding by now. The thing was, he enjoyed good sex. He knew he was good. If this Sara would give him a chance, he bet they could make wild music.

That was how it'd been with Becky. They had fit perfectly, with the exact same touches of kink. She'd been working as a cashier in Denver. She caught his eye with her striking brunette good looks, the alluring swing in her step, the sparkle in her brown eyes, and the enticing curve of her ass.

Hank studied Sara's ass as she walked by, the way her uniform skirt bobbed against that curve...

When he met Becky, he'd just begun driving truck. That was some twenty-five years ago. Hauling feed on a regional route out of Denver, he'd seen her as often as he wanted. He was the only man for her, she'd said. They'd gobbled each other up, got hitched, and she wound up pregnant right away.

Rhonda was a teenager now, barely staying in high school. Hank's stomach clenched when he thought of his daughter. The pie he'd just wolfed down sank like a brick in his stomach.

Dang it, Becky, why did you get sick? Why did you leave us? He tossed his napkin on the table angrily. She'd ruined him. What was there left, after a marriage like theirs?

7

Here he was, aging and balding and horny for this waitress. He couldn't bring himself to ask her out. Not yet. He wanted to be surer. Casual relationships were no good. Not anymore.

It was time to admit it: deep down in his bones, he was lonely as hell. Pretty much an occupational hazard for lone truckers. It wasn't that he didn't like his job. He loved trucking. Hank still hauled livestock feed, now out of Fort Collins. He made a good living at it. But he fantasized about having a female trucking partner. Lots of truckers were husband-and-wife teams. Hank envied them. He really did. He and Becky had planned to do that. But then she got sick.

They'd run out of time.

He wondered what woman would be willing to do his kind of trucking. Hank delivered feed to farmers in southern Wyoming and northern Colorado. He navigated mud holes, walked through cow pastures, and negotiated hog pens to stack feed in barns. He wore cowboy boots because they were comfortable and looked good. Hank always carried two pair of barn boots with him – steel toes and fishing waders – and changed boots when he had to unload.

Lately his back hurt. Another occupational hazard. Thank God the rigs were comfortable now, with good seats. Those first years, his Peterbilt cab had had a hard driver's seat that sent every bump jolting through his spine.

Hank liked the crazy trucking culture, even though it was changing. You never used to see truckers wearing shorts and sandals, for instance. Truckers used to be looked up to. These days too many of them looked like bums or wanna-be rap stars. Hank wouldn't be caught dead wearing shorts or sweat pants when driving truck. Or saggy pants that looked like they were about to fall off.

He liked looking good. In the West, cowboy truckers like Hank enjoyed impressing the ladies at truck stops. So many women were suckers for cowboys, truckers, and biker types. If the guy could dance, better yet.

That was how he'd attracted Becky. Hank was a good dancer.

Women found him irresistible when he led them across a shiny dance floor, two-stepping and doing the cowboy swing. They fell for his strong sense of rhythm and his long, lean body.

He glanced up as Sara leaned slightly forward again, picking up an order. Her skirt dangled over the curve beneath her ass, now and then touching it. He wished he was that skirt, touching it. Hell with it. He could take her dancing, to his favorite place in Cheyenne. She would love it.

"How was the pie?" Sara put his check on the table.

"Best I've had." He licked his lips.

"Good."

"The crust was as good as my mom's."

"Annie, you hear that?" Sara called to the other waitress. "He says your crust is as good as his mom's!"

The one named Annie threw him a grateful smile.

Hank sat there a while, tanking up on coffee. The next time Sara picked up an order, she turned and caught him studying her ass.

Again.

***

"Sara's off today," Annie said, her pencil poised to scribble down his order.

"Oh." Hank kept his face impassive.

"I see how you look at her."

"How's that?"

"Like a hungry coyote, that's how."

He smiled and shrugged. "She's an attractive woman."

"See, here's the thing. Hank, is it?" Annie leaned on the counter, her icy blue eyes drilling into his.

"Yep."

"Sara is off limits."

"Off limits."

9

"Yeah."

"Why is that?"

"That's for her to say. But I'm here to tell you, she's like a daughter to me."

He nodded.

"Sara's been through too much, see. She's kinda … fragile."

"Got it. I'll have a BLT on whole wheat and iced tea, lemon no sugar." He glanced at Annie's scrawny back as she walked away. He'd be damned if he'd let her tell him what to do. He had to admit, though, it was great that she cared enough to protect her friend.

But Annie had only piqued Hank's interest. Now Sara was mysterious, with a secret. Come hell or high water, he would by God find out what the deal was.

CHAPTER 3
RICHARD

He parked across the road, slouched down in his pickup, and opened a beer as he watched his ex-wife through the grill's front windows. Sara laughed at something her snotty friend Annie had just said. Neither of them would recognize this beater truck. Richard was surprised Sara was still in this little backwater burg. He'd figured she would have run home to mama long ago.

He'd been working in the Oregon woods and on fishing boats in Alaska. Then what did he do but get suckered by another sexy woman. Stupid. If only he hadn't married her! It had seemed like a good idea at the time. Man, she had screwed him over but good. He was sick of these bitches thinking they were better than him.

Richard swigged his beer. Yesterday he'd gone in there to talk to her and she'd given him the cold shoulder. Said she couldn't talk when she was at work. Then Annie waited on him. He didn't like the way that stuck-up bitch looked at him. The main thing was, Sara needed to be taken down a peg or two. Or six.

He was just the man to do it.

Richard hated to admit it, but Sara was sure looking good these days. Her face was leaner and prettier. She'd always had a great body. The problem had never been their sex life. While he was teaching her a lesson about how to treat him, he could have some real fun with her.

CHAPTER 4

SARA

She stepped out of the shower, wiped the steam off the mirror, and studied herself. A mammogram had caught the cancer early enough to save her left breast. It could have been so much worse, Sara reminded herself again. She'd dodged so many bullets with this thing. Some women had mastectomies and chemotherapy. She hadn't needed either. Plus, she had just gotten health insurance, three months before the diagnosis. There were a ton of blessings to be thankful for.

Still, the hormone therapy pills were driving her nuts. The doctor said she needed to take them just in case any malignant cells had snuck into her system in her bloodstream. Tamoxifen made her tired, hot, dizzy, achy, and sometimes chilly. Her oncologist said she had to take the damned stuff for another four years. Better safe than sorry, he said.

The radiation scar on the outside of her left breast was a stiff, reddish-brown dent. The nipple area of that breast was darker than her right one. Thank God she'd only needed partial breast radiation. What was it like for women who had their entire breast radiated? Or removed? She shook her head, sighing. Her left breast was now bigger and heavier than the right one. The skin on the breast's outer side was numb. She wasn't supposed to go braless like she used to, but Sara still enjoyed sleeping and lounging around without a bra on.

She'd never been a large-breasted woman. In fact, she'd never cared that much about her breasts. Sara knew she was unusual that way. She'd always been embarrassed about her breasts. Not only were they small, her nipples were inverted. Men could be rude idiots about things like that. She sighed again and rubbed lotion into the scar, massaging it in the circular motion her radiation oncologist had taught her. At least it didn't hurt. Now and then she felt twinges deep inside the breast, but most of the time it felt fine.

What bothered her more than anything these days was a terrible feeling of loneliness. Since that God-awful night with Johnny, she'd shut herself off. She just couldn't bring herself to go out with anyone. But now that her daughter Lexie was on her own, the place felt way too empty. Sara wondered if she should move to a smaller house, or get a housemate. Something.

Of all the times for Richard to show up. Where did he say he was staying? Douglas? That was way too close. Yesterday she'd caught him watching her from his ratty pickup. He'd been drinking beer, of course. She didn't like the look on his face. Finally she went out and talked to him.

Richard said he'd come back to Wyoming to be close to Lexie, who was due to have their first grandchild in three months. That had to be bullshit. Lexie was living in northern Colorado. Why hadn't the son of a bitch moved to Colorado then?

Sara knew how to read that brittle face of his. A face she'd once found handsome. What she'd seen there was anger. She know all too well what a crazy asshole he could be.

Would their daughter even let Richard be around his grandkids? She and Lexie would never forget his mean mouth, beating them down with his sarcastic jabs. Especially when he drank whiskey. The hell of it was, the man was so damned good at making them feel bad. Sara had never understood how Richard managed to make her feel four years old.

All that was years ago.

She'd finally gotten back to her old self.

Lexie was finally happy, too.

Now here he was, surfacing like a phantom shark riding an unwelcome tide. What did he want? Richard was a control freak of the worst kind.

Sara had promised herself that once Lexie was grown up, she would hit the road, finally fly free as a bird. It sounded so simple. But Sara couldn't afford anything. She liked friendly little Chugwater and loved her friends, especially Annie. Lately, though, the walls were closing in. Waitressing didn't pay enough. She was always broke. Her Chevy Aveo was getting old. She kept having car trouble but had no money for a new car. Sara already owed her mechanic monthly payments for fixing the timing belt. She could save money by getting a smaller place. By God, she'd do it. She leaned over the sink and stared at her image in the mirror. "Is this all there is?" she asked.

Her mind raced. She needed a better job but was too broke to take any time off, much less to pay for schooling. Sara wanted to be near her grandchildren, but also wanted to travel. She was stuck, stuck stuck. Not only in her work. In her love life. But, she figured, at least when she was alone her heart was safe.

She looked at herself in the mirror again. Stretching her arm over her head, she felt that little tug. Not bad. The surgeon had done a great job. Sara should keep stretching, though. As a breast cancer survivor, she was supposed to be thankful to be OK. But life made it hard to be grateful. Probably it was that damned hormone therapy making her feel this way.

At the grill she met men who seemed interested. Good men. But Sara froze when anyone asked her out. What if all men reacted like Johnny had to her breast scar? She couldn't take another rejection like that.

She had to find a way to be more careful about which men she trusted.

If she ever trusted a man again.

That moron Johnny had really done a number to her head.

And her heart.

That long-haired cowboy trucker, Hank, filled her mind. Who was it he reminded her of? Sara sat on her bed, leaned back on her hands, and pictured his face, cocking her head. That was it! Tom Selleck! One of her favorites. Hank's eyes reminded her of Selleck's. Those thick eyebrows. Hank was tall but rangy, not muscular like the star. Maybe she could get to know this trucker, but take things nice and slow. The man had kind eyes. She loved his big, strong-looking hands. She'd enjoyed catching him looking at her derriere the other day.

She imagined Hank's huge, rough hands roaming her body. Sara lay back on the bed, running her hands over her silky belly. The thought of him touching her had her hot and wet. She squeezed her legs together and stretched her arms up over her head. This Hank sure did turn her on.

But what if he was another idiot like Johnny?

Sara's eyelids popped open and she sat up. Turning, she again studied her radiation scar in the mirror. Tears sprang to her eyes. The puckered brown mark didn't seem that bad. What the hell was she going to do? Avoid men forever? Never have a sex life again? She was only in her forties. A tear spilled down her cheek. There had to be a way to get past the fear. Sara still craved sex – not as much as she used to, but she still wanted it. Too bad she didn't like women. But no way. She definitely liked men.

Men like Hank.

She took a deep, shuddering breath. Must be the hormone therapy, making her depressed. Time to find a shrink. But how the hell would she pay for something like that?

CHAPTER 5
HANK

Sara was the only waitress at the grill today. Good! Hank decided on the Chugwater Chiliburger Platter. Leaning back, he glanced at the table where Sara was taking three older men's orders.

"I can't believe this 'Fifty Shades of Gray' shit," one was saying.

"I can," another chimed in.

"Have you seen it?" the third one asked.

"Hell, no!" the two men responded in unison.

"What about you, Sara?" that third one asked her.

"Me?" Her head shot up from her order pad, her face turning a flaming shade of pink.

"Yeah, you."

"Um…not yet. But a friend of mine wants me to go see it with her."

"You gonna?"

"I guess… I'm a little curious."

"Hmm," one of the men grunted. "I read it's bored housewives making that thing such a hit."

"That I can believe," another guy muttered.

"Tell me this, young lady," the insistent one said, "do women like to be spanked?"

"Good God, Stan!" another man blurted.

Sara turned on her heel, headed to the kitchen.

"Well…" he mumbled.

"Leave the poor girl alone. Jeez!"

When Sara came to take Hank's order, she wore two red splotches on her cheeks.

He looked into her pretty gray eyes. They were darker than he remembered. Then he realized her pupils were dilated. Weren't dilated pupils a symptom of sexual arousal? Maybe she found spanking exciting. So many did. Hank itched to find out what Sara was into.

He ordered and watched her walk away, wishing he could take her to that "Fifty Shades" movie. He loved light kink, especially ass play. Sad, how many people overlooked the ass as an incredible erogenous zone. They thought it was sinful or deviant. He felt sorry for them.

If Sara didn't know about these things, he could turn her on to whole new areas of ecstasy. That was one thing about his most recent ex: she'd loved to experiment, and had let him explore her whole body. Once she'd tried one of Hank's erotic spankings, she'd been hooked. Spanking her "sweet spot" had made her squirm and moan and beg. A good spanking always made for super-hot sex. He missed that part of his marriage.

But only that part.

He imagined taking this sweet waitress over his knee and having his way with her. After a light spanking, he would tease her, tickle her, explore her, massage her. He would take his sweet time. Again Hank's cock hardened, pressing on the crotch seam of his jeans. What was it about this woman that had him hankerin' to play with her, then mount her like a big ole bull?

It had been a long time since he'd been so hungry for a woman.

Hank was confident that Sara would love having sex with him. He knew what he was doing. If she didn't love it, of course he would stop. He knew how to do things right, how to patiently talk a woman through new experiences, slowly opening her up. He would give Sara so much crazy pleasure, she would never notice that under his cowboy hat he was a balding old fart.

**

He was the only customer left in the place.

"Was everything OK?" she asked, putting his check on the table.

"Best chiliburger ever."

"Good!" Sara fidgeted with her pencil. "We're proud of our Chugwater Chiliburger."

"I can see why." He grinned, wondering if she was really that shy. "I'll probably have another one tomorrow…"

"You're coming back through tomorrow already?"

"I have tomorrow off, but I'm pretty much stuck here."

"Ah."

He took a deep breath. The thing to do was dive in. "I'd like to buy you coffee, or lunch, or dinner…"

She met his eyes, looked away, and bit her plump lower lip. "I have the day off, too."

"Good."

"So … lunch?" She sounded breathless.

"Meet me here at noon."

"I'll be here."

"Great. See you then." He watched the sensuous curve of her bottom lip, red and shiny. He wanted to grab her and take her lovely mouth with his.

But this was neither the time nor the place. Hank reluctantly shifted his gaze up to her eyes and realized she was staring at his lips, her eyes dilated.

**

Their lunch date happened to be on the day of Chugwater's Thirtieth

18

Annual Chili Cook-off. After sandwiches and milk shakes at the Chugwater Soda Fountain, they walked over to the town park where the cook-off was held and strolled around in the warm June sun. The whole town came out for the event's live music, kids' games, and chili.

"I'm a pretty good chili cook myself," Hank told her as he bought souvenir mugs for chili-tasting.

"Me too," she said, her eyes twinkling.

"Hmm. Let's cook chili for each other sometime."

"You're on!"

They tasted all seventeen chili dishes, voted for their favorite, then sat on folding chairs to listen to a county-western band. Hank liked how Sara looked in jeans and cowboy boots. Leaning closer, he caught her lime-and-coconut scent. Nice. He leaned a bit more, touching her shoulder with his.

She didn't pull away.

"Tell me how you ended up in Chugwater," he said.

"I followed my ex-husband here, twenty years ago."

"Ah." Hank cleared his throat. "Where you from?"

"L.A." She seemed to search his face for a reaction.

He waited.

"Richard and I – Richard's my ex – hated Los Angeles. Where did you grow up?"

"Near Colorado Springs."

She nodded, her golden hair bouncing. "Pretty country."

"But too crowded now."

"I hated that about L.A., too. And its superficial culture."

He stretched his long legs in front of him. "That could get irritating all right."

"When Richard found ranch work here, I thought, no way can I stay in this tiny town." She paused, looking at the crowd. "But I love Chugwater. The people here are salt-of-the-earth, the kind who'd give you the shirt off their back."

"Good friends are so important."

"It's true. Sometimes we drive down to Cheyenne for fun, or Denver."

"I've been trucking so long, I'd get restless."

"Sometimes I get that way, especially when I watch you truckers hit the road."

"Really?" He'd had no idea she was interested in trucking. "The road sounds good to you?"

"Yep."

He turned toward her in his chair. "Here I thought you were the settled type."

She laughed. "I have a secret desire to be a trucker."

"Why haven't you pursued it?"

"Money and just…how to get started."

"All those truckers coming into the grill, and none would teach you?"

She lifted her eyebrows. "I'm … picky." Again she watched him for a reaction.

"Well, that's good."

She shrugged.

"How about me?"

"You?" Sara's eyes were dark again.

He winked and gave her a grin. "I'll teach you to be the best trucker this side of the Rockies!"

"You serious?"

"Yep."

She looked dazed.

"What is it?"

"I…I don't know if I can afford to take any time off."

"Oh, that."

"Yeah, that." She chuckled.

"Well, let's worry about that some other time, what do you think?"

"I think that sounds good."

"Dance?" The country band had just started again.

"Love to." She took his hand as she stood.

Her hand was small, silky, and light. Hank was glad the band was playing a slow number. It gave him an excuse to hold her close, to feel how she moved. He held one of her hands. She smelled so good. They were among a dozen or so couples dancing on the grass in front of the makeshift stage. He sensed that her Chugwater friends were watching them, but didn't care. As they swayed, Sara felt good in his arms. She was easy to lead.

"You're a good dancer," he murmured into her ear.

"So are you," she whispered back.

Hank smiled and tucked his nose in her hair, inhaling her coconut scent. They fit. He led her in a slow twirl, gazing into her clear gray eyes.

She met his gaze, her eyes shining.

Hank brought her back into his arms, swayed for a few beats, and dipped her.

Sara's eyes widened in surprise, but she was smiling.

Again he brought her back into his arms, this time leading her in several turns.

When the song ended, they applauded the band. Neither of them made a move to leave the dance area.

The musicians broke into a lively two-step.

Again holding one of his hands, she moved her shoulders with his as they danced a counter-clockwise circle. Only six other couples were dancing, so they had plenty of room.

Sara waved at one of the other couples, laughing, and looked up at him. Her eyes were smiling, her face flushed as she moved with him.

He could not get enough of this woman. Turning her so that they two-stepped side by side, Hank rested his right hand on her right shoulder. She smoothly followed along, holding his left hand with hers. He could do this all day. When he knew her better, they could do more intimate versions of this dance, their hands joined at their hips, or arms around each other.

They had plenty of time. Hank was sure of it.

He brought her back into the face-to-face hold and gave her a quick twirl as the song ended.

Again they applauded, staying right where they were.

He could tell she was loving it.

The band played another slow dance. Hank led her again, this time tucking her hand in his next to his chest. They swayed side to side in bigger moves, warming to each other.

She suddenly stiffened.

He pulled back to look at her.

Sara was staring at something over his shoulder, her smile gone and fear in her shadowed eyes.

"What is it?"

"Richard's over there watching us."

"Richard...your ex?"

"Yep," she murmured in his ear. "Let's get out of here."

He nodded, holding her hand as they made their way back to their chairs. A barrel-chested blonde man rushed up to Sara. Hank felt her cringe just before she dropped his hand.

"Honey, how 'bout a dance?" the guy blurted. He smelled like a brewery. His tattered blue shirt was cut off at the shoulders, showing tan, muscular arms.

"I don't think so, Richard," she said, her voice cold.

"C'mon, it'll be like old times." Richard tried to grab her hand.

Hank wondered how often people said no to this guy. He was one of those heavily muscled types, probably played football in his youth. His neck was wider than his head, sloping into massive shoulders.

Sara was backing away.

The guy kept moving closer to her, a mean look in his bloodshot eyes.

Hank inserted himself between them. "We were just leaving," he said, keeping his voice calm.

People were watching. A few of the men edged closer, apparently ready to help handle Richard.

Hank figured the man must have quite a history around here.

"Who the hell are you?" Richard slurred.

"This is Hank—" Sara began.

"I don't give a shit!" Richard looked Hank up and down.

"Richard, please," she pleaded.

Hank took a step toward Richard. "The lady wants to leave."

"The LADY?" Richard followed them as Hank led Sara away.

Hank abruptly turned, causing Richard to crash into him. "Yes, the lady," he said firmly.

A tall, red-haired cowboy stepped up. "Come on, buddy, I'll buy ya a beer," he told Richard.

"Hey, Jeff, now you're talkin'." He stumbled off with his friend.

Hank watched him go.

Richard turned back and shot him a nasty look. It was a malicious, squinting glance that clearly said, "We're not finished."

CHAPTER 6
SARA

She sat on her bed and brushed her hair. Sara was tired, but in a good way. Hank had been perfect, the way he'd handled Richard. He'd been calm, cool, and strong. Again she felt that pull in her groin. She smiled to herself. Hank turned her on more than ever. It was her favorite quality in a man – quiet, gentle strength. He was strong enough to be gentle.

He was not afraid of Richard, even though her ex was much more muscular. But then sometimes wiry guys could surprise you with their physical strength.

Hank had fit right in with the small town crowd today. He'd looked sharp as usual, even with his beat-up straw cowboy hat. He'd left his hat on when they danced. She liked that hat. It had character.

The main thing was, Sara'd been able to unwind and be herself with Hank. There was something about the Flying Bison Grill that made her feel self-conscious with the customers. She wondered if he was serious about teaching her to drive his semi. A CDL could be her way out of always being broke. Maybe she could have it all – the road, better paychecks, and visits with Lexie and her grandchild.

And Hank. Could she have Hank?

Loud knocking on the front door startled her. Who could that be? It was late. Could it be Hank? She grabbed her robe from the bed.

"Open up!" Richard bellowed.

Her heart sank. Of course it wasn't Hank. She threw on her robe, tying the belt tightly around her waist.

"Richard?"

"Let me in, Sara."

He sounded loaded. "It's late." He'd been gone for years. She'd prayed he would stay gone, hoping she was rid of him for good. But here he was, probably stinking of whiskey.

"I just want to talk to you."

"I'm tired."

"Just for a minute?"

He sounded pathetic. It would be good if they could get along, for Lexie's sake. She unlocked the door.

Richard rushed in. He smelled like a distillery and his face was puffy, with dark circles under his eyes. His work pants were dirty, and she could smell stale cigarette smoke on him.

"What is it, Richard?"

"I had to see you." He swayed on his feet.

"After all this time?"

"I don't know..." He scratched his head.

"I don't know either."

"You sure look pretty." Richard looked her up and down.

Sara's heart leapt to her throat. "We'll talk tomorrow."

"This is nice," he said, fingering the lapel of her green chenille robe. "Mmm."

"Come on," she said, leading him by the elbow toward the door. "We'll talk tomorrow, ok?"

Richard grabbed her hand from his arm, yanked her into the living room, and pulled her down to the sofa next to him.

Sara's mind flashed to that night right after the divorce. She'd jolted awake, her scream muffled by a big hand. Richard had broken in. She knew damned well what a bully he could be. Shit! Why had she unlocked the door just now?

His beefy hand gripped the back of her neck. His other hand was on her knee, as if taking ownership.

She pushed his big shoulders away as hard as she could. He was too strong, though. Her mind darted around like a frightened rabbit. Get to the kitchen, to the knives. The cayenne pepper. The smell of him turned her stomach. She twisted her face away from him.

Richard wrapped his hand in her hair and yanked her head back around, forcing her to look at his angry, red face. "Who do you think you are?" He ran his other hand up the outside of her thigh.

"What do you mean?" she whispered, pushing his hand off her leg with both of her hands. Where was her phone?

"You bitch!" He grabbed her wrists, pinned them over her head, and held them with one hand.

She yelped.

"You know damned well what I mean!" He leaned in, sniffing her neck, his other hand stroking her jaw.

"No, I don't."

"You think you can just dump me and hook up with other guys?"

She stared at him, her mind racing. That night he'd broken in, he'd been all tough talk, no action. Even then he hadn't hurt Sara. It was all about power for him.

"I'll kill you! And I'll kill any bastard you hook up with, like that skinny cowboy you were with today."

"Richard…" He was too much of a coward to really do anything.

"SHUT UP!"

Maybe she could reach the lamp, hit him over the head with it. She tried to wiggle her wrists loose, but he was holding her in a tight, bruising grip.

"I've seen you with those guys at the grill, too." He stroked the side of her neck.

"What guys? Come on—"

He wrapped his burly hand around her throat and squeezed just a little. "IF I CAN'T HAVE YOU, NO ONE CAN."

Sara swallowed. Time. She needed time. She knew him inside and out. Maybe if she pretended to want him. But how to get him out of her house right now, tonight? Her eyes teared up.

"I don't want to hurt you, Sara," he whispered, moving his hand from her throat. He slipped it inside her robe and rubbed her right nipple.

She remembered how much he hated having sex when she had her period. Sara forced herself to relax against the sofa, deliberately arching her back and wiggling her hips as if turned on.

"You always did like that…" He pinched her nipple lightly.

"Mmmm."

He kneaded her breast.

"Oooh." She writhed for him. "Babe, I want to touch you…"

"Promise to be a good girl?" He flicked her nipple again, and she arched.

"I'm always good."

"Yeah, sex was never a problem."

She smiled her best sexy smile.

Richard finally let go of her wrists, pulling her onto his lap.

She leaned against his big chest as if she liked it.

"Got any whiskey, darlin'?" His thick hands moved down to her ass.

"Sorry, babe."

He slapped her ass and grinned. "I got more in the truck." He spanked her again, a little harder. "Mmm, sexy thing…"

She ran her hands along his shoulders and back. How exactly was she going to manage this?

As if reading her mind, his mood shifted like quicksilver. "You should NOT have left me!" He slapped her ass, really hard this time.

She jumped. "OW!" That one had hurt. He was scary strong. Stronger than ever. Crazier than ever, too. Damn. Sara wanted him

27

out of here, quickly. "Richard…" she cooed, rubbing the back of his thick neck.

His beady eyes narrowed as he waited for her to go on.

"Babe, I've missed you." She moved her hips rhythmically, the way she knew he loved. His big hand was still warm on her ass. "Let's fuck, wild, you know, like old times."

His eyes widened. "You serious?" he asked, incredulous.

"Yes," she purred in her breathiest voice. "But…"

"But what?"

"I have my period."

"Shit!" Richard dropped both of his hands from her as if she were poison.

"Let's get together in a few days."

"OK."

"Cool."

"I'm gonna rock you good, mama. I've learned a few things…"

"We'll break the bed like we did that time, remember?"

"How could I forget?" He eased her off his lap and onto the sofa.

Sara took a deep breath. Thank God Richard was stupid enough to believe her.

"Guess I'll get going," he mumbled.

"Good night," she said, managing to sound sweet.

He stumbled across the front yard and climbed into his rusty pickup, muddled but obviously happy about the prospect of fucking her.

Sara stood in the open door and watched him drive away, then locked herself inside again.

There was her phone, on the kitchen table. It was late, but the lawyer had told her to call whenever she needed to. This definitely qualified, she thought, shaking her head as she punched in his number.

She couldn't afford this.

More lawyer bills. Shit!

There was no way around it, though. She needed legal advice, and maybe a restraining order. Now.

CHAPTER 7

HANK

He glanced over at the passenger seat, where Sara sipped Diet Dr. Pepper through a straw. She was decked out for a Saturday night of dancing in Cheyenne, her turquoise tank top and silver necklace sparkling in the low evening sun. Her skin was golden. Hank had to force himself to keep his eyes on the interstate in front of him. This was the first time he'd seen her in her black cowboy hat, black jeans, silver and black belt, and black boots. Man, she looked sharp. Like a cowgirl ready for anything.

His cock leaped at the sight of her. Whoa, he told himself. He sensed that it wouldn't take much to scare her off. He stole another quick look as she sipped her drink, the plump curves of her wet lips shining gold in the sun. His cock shot up again. Dang it. He'd better think about something else.

"Where did you drive today?" she asked, turning toward him in her seat.

"A short run up to Casper. I'm deadheading home – that's what we call hauling an empty trailer." Sara could have followed him to Cheyenne in her car, but this was more fun. He'd have to bring her home, but it was only forty-five miles from Cheyenne to Chugwater.

"Your truck's amazing." She touched the fancy Kenworth dash.

"Thanks. I like it."

"I can see why. So, where are we going again?"

"The Desperado."

She nodded. "I had a drink there once, but it was during the week so it was pretty quiet."

"I guess Saturday night is crazy there."

"I'm glad to get out of town. Richard's been bugging me."

"He's bugging you?"

"He keeps showing up at the grill. And a few other places."

"What does he want?"

"Who knows?" Sara shrugged her beautiful shoulders.

"Yeah, I hear you."

"I'm ready to have some fun, just forget about all that."

"Good!"

"I tell you, Hank, sometimes I feel like running away."

He noticed a worry line between her eyebrows that he'd never seen before. "As long as you run away with me," he teased, imagining whisking her off. He wished he could rescue her from her problems. Whoa, he scolded himself again. Slow your ass down. Why did he keep getting ahead of himself with this woman?

"Don't tempt me," she teased back.

"Hmmm." Hank chuckled. "I have to make a quick stop over here."

Sara watched as he parked and unhooked the trailer in a feed dealer parking lot.

It was only a few blocks to the Desperado. "Let's lock your purse and jacket in here," Hank suggested, "so we can dance the night away with no worries."

Sara began to put some bills in her jeans pocket.

"You won't need that," he told her.

"But—"

"But nothing. I'm buying."

"Well, all righty then." She put the money back and flashed a grin at him. "Mr. Big Bucks."

31

He laughed, climbing out of the rig.

Sara surprised him by climbing out before he could help her.

The independent type, he thought. As they strolled hand-in-hand across the saloon's massive parking lot, the red sun was sinking into the horizon. "Wow, this place is crazy big," he commented.

"Crazy fun, too, I've heard." She gave his hand a little squeeze.

He squeezed back.

They wandered through the smoky club, still hand-in-hand, taking in the live honky tonk music, the massive dance floor, and a crowd of people line dancing. Off to the side, folks were playing pool, foosball, and darts. Others were gambling. In one corner, women were riding two mechanical bulls surrounded by mattresses. The other corners had big screen TVs with sports games on. The tables in those sections were packed with loud, beer-swilling sports fans.

"It's a regular three-ring circus," Hank said.

"I love it!" Sara smiled. "Nothing like a real honky-tonk on a Saturday night."

They explored the two upper floors. Each floor had a busy bar, with waterfalls under the stairs.

"This looks great," Hank said, leading her onto a big patio where someone had lit a fire in a brick fire ring.

"Ooh, look at that."

The sunset was painting the high clouds overhead with streaks of red and purple. "Nice!"

They sat near the fire and drank their beers.

He moved his chair close to hers and put his arm around her shoulder.

Sara took her cowboy hat off and rested her head against his arm. "You smell good. Aramis?"

"Yep. I like your scent, too."

"Lime, coconut and verbena."

"What the heck is verbena?"

"An herb, I think."

Hank ran his nose along her upper arm and inhaled. "Mmm, good enough to eat." He nuzzled her shoulder. Damned if she didn't break out in goose bumps. Hank stroked her bare upper arm.

Sara shivered.

A sensitive one, he thought. Promising. For God's sake, make polite conversation, he told himself. But he couldn't keep his hands off her. What was it about this woman? "Let's go in and watch the dancers," he suggested, grabbing her hand.

"OK."

The place was really jumping. People were jammed into the saloon, smoking, drinking, laughing, and dancing. The band was belting out a lively two-step number, an old country classic. Hank and Sara found a spot where they could lean against the bar and watch. The couple next to them threw down tequila shots and headed back to the dance floor.

"We have a request, people," the band's front man announced. "The Cotton Eyed Joe!"

The crowd roared. As the fiddle tune began, everyone grabbed a partner. Hank and Sara were swept up as people surged onto the massive dance floor. She looked spooked.

"Just hang onto me, ok?" he hollered.

Sara nodded mutely.

The crowd formed lines like spokes of a wheel. As they danced, the wheel rotated. Then the dancers stopped and kicked twice, hollering "bullshit!" and shuffling backwards. Then they travelled forward again.

Hank and Sara danced with their arms around each other's waists. She looked up at him, pushed her cowboy hat up, and laughed. God, she looked good.

The fiddle tune sped up. It was wild as the line dancers tried to keep up with the rhythm.

"This is crazy!" Sara giggled again, her face beaming.

"I love it!" He loved watching her, too.

With hoots and hollers, the dance finished. Almost everyone left the dance floor.

Hank and Sara stayed put as the band broke into a slow dance.

"Shall we?" he asked.

"Absolutely."

She moved into his arms naturally. She belonged in his arms, Hank thought, leading her in a slow turn.

***

"Mmmm." Sara kissed him in the moonlight that poured through the cabin's skylight. They sat on his double bed, since the cab had nowhere else where they could sit together comfortably. "This is nice," she said, looking up at the sleeper's high, curved ceiling.

"I like it," he mumbled into her hair. "It's homey."

She nodded. "I can see that. Must be amazing to be on the road—"

"Shut up and kiss me," he muttered. A balmy breeze wafted in through the open windows as he held her neck and went in for another kiss. Sara tasted sweet, like mint.

She rubbed the back of his neck and kissed him back with enthusiasm. Then she accidentally knocked his cowboy hat off.

Crap. Now she'd see his balding head. Damn it.

"Oooh," Sara cooed, running her hands over his thin hair. "Look at you without your hat." Her words were slightly slurred.

"Are you tipsy?" he teased.

"Hell, yes." She giggled. "Your fault for buying tequila shots. But we're talking about your hair."

"Must we?" He grinned at her. Those silver necklaces of hers flashed in the moonlight.

"This is the first time I've seen your hair, Mr. Handsome."

"It had to happen sometime."

"What are you talking about?" She leaned her head back and gazed up at him.

"Well—"

"Bald men are the sexiest."

"No way," he said.

"Way!"

Hank chuckled. "You're crazy, but I love it."

"I've heard bald men have more testosterone."

"Yeah?"

"Yeah. And that makes them sexier, right?"

The angles of her face were gorgeous in the blue moonshine. Maybe she really was perfect for him. He shrugged, tossing his hat to the foot of the bed. Again she ran her hands over his thin salt-and-pepper hair, which was still tied in a ponytail. Man, her hands on him felt so good. There went his cock, leaping to life again. His cock had a mind of its own. It was hell-bent to get inside her. As they kissed, one of his hands brushed against her left breast.

Sara flinched and pulled back. She pushed his arms away, suddenly cold.

"What?" he asked. What had he done?

She bolted from the bed and sat in the passenger seat, which was swiveled toward the sleeper.

He stared at her. "What's wrong, Sara?"

"Sorry," she whispered, turning the seat away from him and facing the windshield.

"What happened?"

She was silent as she gazed out the passenger window.

He could feel her struggling, trying to speak.

"I just can't," she finally managed to say, her voice thin.

***

As he drove her home, he reviewed the evening. If he'd done something wrong, he had no idea what it was. They were almost at her place. He had to get her to talk before she bolted into her house. "Sara?"

She looked at him.

"If it's something I did, I'm sorry."

"No," she whispered. "It's not you. It's me."

"I won't let you push me away."

She nodded, her eyes shining.

"I won't give up on you."

Sara nodded again, swallowing hard.

"I have tomorrow off …"

She waited.

"Let's do something tomorrow."

"Really? Even after—"

"I'm not that easily spooked." He pulled up in front of her house.

She gave him a slow smile. "I have to work till four."

"How 'bout I pick you up here, about 4:30?"

"OK," she whispered.

He climbed out and helped her down.

"Sorry I ruined things tonight…" she began.

He pulled her to him. "Nothing is ruined, you got that?" Hank held her tight, his heart pounding. "I'm a patient guy."

She finally relaxed into him, slipping both of her arms around his neck.

He kissed her for a full minute, gently at first. Then insistently.

"Tomorrow," she murmured when they came up for air.

Hank watched her go down her front walkway.

Before letting herself in the front door, she waved.

He waved back. Once she was inside, he climbed back into the semi. If anything, he was more hooked now. What was her big secret? What was it that had her so terrified? Now he not only wanted that body of hers, he really did yearn to rescue her from whatever problems she had.

Hank glanced back at Sara's house. What was that? Something had moved from the black shadows. Now there was no movement. He could have sworn something was there. He watched for a minute. Nothing. He must have imagined it, he thought, putting the truck in gear and pulling away from the curb.

***

Hank lay there in the dark. If only Sara were here with him. It could be fun, teaching her to drive his rig. What would it be like to have a trucking partner like her? Ooh, baby. If she were here right now, he would have her wear her waitress uniform. He would have her stand next to him. He'd caress those gorgeous legs, running his hands under her pink skirt. He would stroke her ass though her silk panties. He would slowly stroke her inner thighs, higher and higher, pushing her legs open. He would grab the crotch of her panties, roughly, making her gasp as he pulled them down to her knees. "Hold your skirt up," he would tell her.

She would do it, licking her lips seductively.

He would run his hand back up her inner thighs. He'd stroke her cleft and plunge a couple of fingers into the heat of her tight, wet cunt. "Now, my beauty, bend over the bed for me," he would tell her.

She would obey wordlessly.

Finally he'd be behind her, hands on her ass, spreading her cheeks. He'd press her waist down, sending her ass high in the air the way he liked. He'd rub his cock against her hot crease. Then he would fuck her deep and hard, plunging all the way in and out, his cock harder than it had ever been before.

"Christ!" He exploded into his hand.

CHAPTER 8

SARA

She tossed and turned, cursing herself for freezing up like that with Hank. She did want him so. Sara was drawn to him like she'd never been drawn to anyone, ever. She turned over and planted her feet on the bed. What was it about him? Quiet strength. That was a lot of it. Hank had nothing to prove, but would do whatever was necessary. An in-charge guy. The real deal. It turned her on. Sara had always fantasized about bossy men, forceful lovers. They weren't exactly rape fantasies, were they? She wondered. She was always submissive. She felt that familiar pang of guilt. Of course she wouldn't really want to be raped! But that sweet bossiness, from a man she wanted. That was the best.

After the sex, she would go back to being equal. She'd read that this was a common female sex fantasy because it allowed a woman to indulge her femininity, but still embrace feminism. She grinned into the dark bedroom, remembering how Hank looked without his cowboy hat. Was she crazy to find bald men sexy? There was that actor Yul Brenner, and the guy in Star Trek. All she knew was that to her, Hank was white-hot sexy. She craved his touch.

It scared her. It wasn't just the radiation scar thing. Hank touched her deep in her heart. It was exciting, their potential connection. But it scared the crap out of her.

She imagined his big hands all over her. Sara touched her

breast scar, tears rolling down her temples. She had to trust Hank. Either that or go crazy. He was a great guy.

But she'd thought Johnny was a great guy too. What a jerk. Johnny'd been so hot, then so cold. She'd never felt so humiliated.

She was not about to let that happen again.

And Richard. What was it with her and men anyway? She sighed deeply, turning onto her side. He was back like a bad virus. In a couple of days Richard would come around again, expecting the hot sex she'd promised. Her stomach twitched and her heart began pounding. She'd better figure something out. It was a dangerous game, lying to Richard. She swallowed hard. If he found out she'd lied about having her period, she hated to think what he would do. Damn. She'd thought he was out of her life forever. That had been a naïve notion.

She shook her head and sat up, more awake than ever. Walking to the bathroom, she pinned her hair up and turned on the shower. Sara got in, leaned back, and let the hot water pummel her chest. She ran her hands over her nipples, imagining Hank in the shower with her. She soaped up, running her hand between her legs and finding her sensitive clit. He would lather her all over, pin her against the shower wall, and thrust her thighs apart with his knees. He would snake his fingers through her hair, pull her head back, and sink his teeth into her shoulder. He would lift her as if she weighed nothing, wrap her legs around his waist, and take her, pinning her hard against the wall as he plunged again and again.

"GOD!" Sara shrieked, her knees buckling from her orgasm.

CHAPTER 9
RICHARD

He parked in front of the grill, hungry for a big Sunday breakfast. There she was, in the sunny window, serving pancakes to a family. Richard scratched his chin stubble, watching her. Was she finished with her damned period yet? He couldn't wait to nail her, bang her till she begged him to stop.

When he walked through the door, Sara was talking to a hefty-looking man at the counter. She refilled his coffee cup and threw her head back, laughing and touching his arm.

Richard froze, his scalp prickling as he balled up his fists. Who the hell was this guy? Sara was his and his alone. That's the way it was, the way it would always be.

Sara spotted him. A worried frown replaced her smile. "Good morning!"

He heard her forced cheeriness.

"Coffee, Richard?"

He planted himself next to the guy, who was drinking his coffee. "Who the hell is this?" Richard watched the big guy put his cup down and turn to face him.

The guy smiled at him.

He'd wipe that grin off his fucking face.

"This is my friend Ben—"

"Your friend, huh?" With lightning speed Richard threw a punch, his right fist landing in the guy's eye.

Ben lunged out of his seat and barreled into Richard, tackling him. Customers scattered out of the way.

"STOP IT!" Sara was screaming from behind the counter.

The men got in a few good jabs as they rolled around on the floor, knocking into chairs and tables.

"STOP!" Sara yelled.

Ben was on top of him.

God, the guy weighed a ton.

Ben thumped him hard with a straight right to the nose.

Richard heard the crunch. Whoa, the guy could pack a wallop.

"Had enough?" Ben growled.

Richard couldn't answer, shocked by the sudden pain shooting from his nose into his forehead. "Owww! Fuck!" He could feel warm blood pouring from his nostrils and down into his mouth. "Shit!" he hollered, holding his nose. "God damn!!"

CHAPTER 10

SARA

Max sat her down in his little office off the kitchen. "Sorry, but I cannot have this kind of thing," he was saying. "Just take some time off, straighten out your life…"

"But I can't afford time off," she protested.

"I'm not asking you," the boss insisted. "I'm telling you."

Tears sprang into her eyes. Shit! She hated crying when she wanted to look strong. "Can't you just '86' him?" she asked in a small, quaking voice.

"He's already 86'd."

"Oh."

He leaned forward, elbows on his desk. "No worries," Max said. "You're not fired."

Sara nodded mutely. She didn't trust herself to speak. She might burst into embarrassing sobs. Easy for him to say no worries. Money was always a huge worry for her. Things were already tight, but now it would be downright scary.

"We like you, Sara. We don't want to lose you."

That was something, she supposed. Stupid Richard! What a moron, coming in here and picking a fight. God! He was still messing up her life, even after all these years.

She could kill him. She really could.

CHAPTER 11

HANK

"She's not here," Annie said when he stopped by the grill.

That was a surprise. "Is she OK?"

The older waitress nodded. "The boss sent her home."

Hank lifted his eyebrows.

"Sara's ex picked a fight with one of our regulars."

Hank just shook his head.

"Jerk got his nose broken," Annie added with a smirk.

***

Sara opened her door and fell into Hank's arms. She held him tight around his waist and buried her face in his shirt.

"Don't look at me!" she wailed.

"Why?"

"My eyes are puffy." She sniffed.

He kissed the top of her head. She seemed taller. Then he noticed her feet, clad in strappy high heels. He'd never seen her in shoes like this. God, they were sexy. They showed off Sara's tanned toes and delicate high arch. "Wow!"

"What?"

"Nice shoes, lady."

"I just got 'em. You caught me trying 'em on."

"I love them!"

"Thanks," she said without enthusiasm.

"Annie told me what happened," he murmured. "Seems unfair that you have to take time off."

Sara finally looked up at him, her big eyes red from crying. "I know."

He stroked the top of her head. Her golden brown hair was silky.

"I can't believe that bastard Richard is still screwing things up for me. Max just wants me to get the situation in hand."

"I guess that's understandable."

"Yeah."

"You probably don't feel like going out after all."

Sara took a deep breath. "Actually, I do. I need to get my mind off this stuff."

He sensed that she wanted to say more, but somehow couldn't do it.

"Where did you say we're going?" she asked.

"Guernsey."

"What's in Guernsey?"

"You'll see. Bring your swimsuit and a towel."

"OK."

"Oh, and wear those high heels, ok? But bring some walking shoes to change into."

***

"I love this place," Hank said, offering Sara his hand. "Imagine the settlers walking the Oregon Trail for weeks and weeks."

"Wow!" She stared at the five-feet-deep wagon ruts gouged into the white ridge. "I can't believe I've never come here before. What kind of rock is this?"

"Sandstone, I think." It was astounding how well-preserved the old trail was here at Guernsey State Park.

"The pioneers came through here in the 1840s, right?"

"Yep." He followed her as she walked along the deeply rutted historic trail. "Every wagon that went west had to cross this ridge right here."

Sara sat down with her feet in a deep rut, and ran her hands on the sun-bleached rock trail. "Amazing," she murmured.

"It really is."

They wandered along the old trail for a while, then went to Register Cliff, where settlers had inscribed their names. The "signatures" were still clearly visible, declaring the exact dates when the emigrants had passed this rock on their way west.

"Whew!" Hank wiped his brow. "It's hot."

"Getting that way," she agreed.

"I have cold drinks in the cooler."

"Great."

"And I know a place where we can cool off."

At the reservoir, Sara took his breath away when she came out of the ladies room. He'd never seen her in a swimsuit before. Her body was crazy beautiful, the way her waist narrowed and her hips curved. The purple one-piece suit was cut out at the side, with ties at her hips and behind her lovely neck. Hank wanted to reach out and untie those ties. Plus, she had those sparkly high heels on again. Damn! He would sit her down on a blanket on the grass and slowly take those high heels off, then rub her feet, maybe suck her toes...

High bluffs surrounded the park, jutting up dramatically from the prairie. They blocked the wind. There were plenty of folks swimming and water skiing. They spread their blanket.

"Sit," he told her.

"Yes, sir," she teased, arching her eyebrows at him.

"I want to check these out," Hank said, exploring the high heels. He ran his fingers along her high arches, to her ankles, and down to her toes.

Sara giggled and snatched her feet away.

"Ticklish?"

"A little."

He took one of her feet and ran his finger inside the high heel straps, then slowly unbuckled the shoe and slid it off her slender foot. He rubbed the bottom of her foot.

"Anyone ever told you you're weird, Hank Werner?" She smiled.

"Just every day, Sara Cooke." He gave her other foot the same treatment.

She sighed. "Well, you're in luck."

"How's that?"

"I adore having my feet touched."

He grinned and set the high heels next to each other on the blanket.

They ran into the water and swam to the dock. She was gorgeous, her hair sleek and droplets of water glistening on her face. Hank held her, his hands playing with the little cutout parts of her suit. Her arms went up around his neck and his fingers went to one of the little ties at her hips. He heard her gasp, and surprised her by running his hand under the tie instead of undoing it. His hand roamed to her fine ass. He cupped one cheek, pressed her to him firmly, and leaned in for a kiss.

Sara kissed him back, her plump lips opening slightly.

He took her delicious mouth, exploring her tongue with his.

She moaned so faintly he could barely hear it, and met his tongue with hers.

Both of his hands were on her ass, lifting her into him as they necked like teenagers.

Her hands were in his hair.

Her body pressed into his was a perfect fit. He loved her heat against his stiffening cock in the cool water. He moaned as she rubbed his ears. He ran his mouth along her jaw and down the side of her neck. "Sara," he whispered.

"Yes..." she whispered into his ear.

"I want you."

"Me too." Her hands were on his shoulders now.

"I like you."

"Me too." She gave him a sexy smile.

"What are we waiting for?"

"Um, well, nothing," she mumbled. "I just like to take things slow."

"Right." He caressed her ass again, then moved his hands back to her waist. "Like I said, I'm a patient guy."

"Good. You hungry?"

"Well, yes." He grinned.

"For food, I mean."

"Oh, that."

They swam a little more and got out. Sitting on the blanket, they let the hot sun warm their skin as they ate sandwiches.

"Now I'm free to go with you in your semi," Sara said between bites.

"Mmmm," he nodded, his mouth full.

"I mean, since I can't go to work anyway."

"Right."

"Hank, I need to get out of town, away from Richard."

He nodded again. "He seems dangerous."

She swallowed.

"I'm worried about you, Sara."

She tossed her wet hair and leaned back on her arms. "He's gotten worse since we were together."

"I can't imagine you ever married to someone like that."

"I know." She lifted her face to the sun, her eyes closed.

Hank studied the planes of her face as she sunned herself, realizing how much he cared about her. She was so easy to be with, so lovely. So vulnerable. A surge of protectiveness coursed through him, and he balled his fists. If anything happened to this woman, he hated to think what he would do to that crazy bastard Richard.

"Anyway," she was saying, "I would love to learn to drive

the eighteen-wheeler, if you don't mind teaching me…"

"No problem. It'll be fun." The word "fun" didn't really describe what they would have in his cab. In his sleeper. He'd have her put on that swimsuit and those high, high heels. He'd untie those ties, slowly bare her feet, and have his way with her. He glanced again at those strappy shoes sitting on the blanket. They even had a delicate little chain that hung between a couple of the straps.

"Great! I'll owe you…"

"Yes, you will," he teased, nudging her shoulder with his. He leaned over and nuzzled her ear.

Sara laughed him off, refusing to be distracted. "A CDL would mean I could move on, and make a better living."

"I think it'll be great for you. Just get a manual, study it, and take the written test. Then you'll be ready for driving lessons."

"I'm excited!" She wrapped her arms around his neck and gave him a long, deep kiss, running her tongue around his tongue.

To Hank it felt like a promise of things to come.

"It shouldn't take you more than a few days to get the written test done," he told her when they finally ended their kiss. "This week I'm doing short, local runs. I'll be around."

"Great!"

"Here's my number," he said, handing her a business card. "Call me whenever."

"OK."

"I hate the idea of you being alone with Richard around." He wished he could stay with her himself.

"Great minds think alike," she said, smiling. "Annie's gonna stay with me."

"Good!" He jumped up and pulled her to her feet.

Holding hands, they ran down the dock and leaped into the water.

CHAPTER 12
RICHARD

Richard's nose hurt. It was swollen, bent, and bruised. He couldn't breathe right, and one nostril kept running.

"Shit!" he muttered, leaning toward the bathroom mirror to look. The damned swelling should have gone down by now, especially with the ice packs he'd been holding on it. Now he'd have to get his friggin' nose x-rayed. Tylenol didn't even touch the pain.

He hated spending money on doctors. But he decided to get the x-ray done right away. He wanted to be in top form to give Sara a sound screwing. Sexy damned bitch.

Someone knocked on his door.

Richard padded over to the door, where a deputy stood waiting.

"This is for you," the lawman said, handing him a thick envelope.

Richard tore it open. "An order for protection," he read aloud. "A restraining order to protect victims of <u>domestic abuse</u>. Domestic abuse?"

"I just deliver it," the deputy mumbled.

Richard scratched his greasy head.

"If I were you, I'd steer clear of Chugwater."

Richard nodded, acting mellow. He just wanted the guy gone. Once the deputy left, he went in, leaned on the kitchen counter, and read the entire document. It covered physical abuse, <u>sexual abuse</u>, and verbal threats of abuse to a former spouse.

"Shit!" He kicked the flimsy coffee table across the room and collapsed on the sofa. "Ow!" Was his nose splitting in half or what?

That bitch! Probably got his address from their daughter.

He opened his last beer and took a big drink. That night at her place. Had she lied to him then? Or was this order because of the fight at the grill?

Either way, he was screwed.

He'd sure as hell make Sara pay for this. He was gonna fuck her up good.

Richard glanced at the living room clock. Time for a whiskey run, before the liquor store closed.

CHAPTER 13

SARA

She sat in the Cheyenne DMV office, watching the woman mark up the exam form. Sara busied herself, pushing her cuticles up. Maybe she should have taken more than one day to study the manual. God knows she had plenty of time now.

Thanks to that damned Richard.

No. Wrong. She didn't have time. She needed to get moving on this CDL thing so she could get the hell out of town for a while.

"Miss Cooke?" The woman smiled and waved her over.

That smile had to be a good sign, Sara thought, perching on the chair in front of the woman's desk.

"You did well, honey."

"Oh, good!" Sara's right hand went to her chest, where her heart was pounding.

"Here's your learner's permit. Congratulations, and be safe out there, OK?"

"Absolutely. Thank you so much!"

She was finally on her way to becoming a trucker! Sara sat in her car, staring at her test paper and shivering at the thought of Hank teaching her to drive his purple rig. What was it they called Kenworths? K-whoppers? If he could just take her on the road right away. She'd never felt so desperate to get out of town.

She knew Richard. His stupid broken nose had nothing to do with her, but she'd bet good money he'd take it out on her. Then there was the restraining order. He'd be livid when he got that thing, especially since she'd promised to have sex with him.

Shuddering, Sara held her head in her hands. If only she hadn't promised him that. She hadn't known how else to get him out of her house that night. What if he was crazy enough to demand sex, even with a broken nose and a restraining order? She swallowed hard. The safest thing would be to let him have his way.

The thought of it made her stomach lurch.

She would have to act like she wanted him. Maybe if she pretended he was Hank…

Sara took Hank's card from her wallet and punched the numbers in.

He picked up in the middle of the second ring. "Yo!"

"I passed!"

"Good deal!"

"Let's celebrate."

"Sounds good. I'm north of Chugwater now, have to unload … how 'bout I come to your place?"

"Great! I'll make dinner."

"Can't wait, sweet lady."

***

Hank stood behind her, his hands on her waist, as she stirred the homemade refried beans. Everything was ready. He leaned forward and inhaled the steam from the beans.

"Mmmm, I love Mexican food!"

"Good! Me too." Sara also loved his muscular thighs pressed against hers.

He nuzzled her cheek.

Tonight he smelled of leather and clean hay. She had deliberately worn her shortest, tightest cutoffs, her favorite green halter top, and the new strappy high heels he loved. One of her friends used to call heels like these "fuck me" shoes. With Hank behind her, breathing on her bare shoulders, she understood why they were called that. All she would have to do is lean forward slightly... The coarse denim of Hank's jeans rubbed against the backs of her legs, and Sara was glad she'd splurged on the crazy shoes. She wanted him to want her. The shoes helped. Those hard thighs of his, in those jeans. Those lean arms wrapped around her waist. Her knees turned to jelly, her center on fire again. She took a swig of beer.

He shifted his hands down over her belly. "Let's have another beer before we eat."

"OK." Her own voice sounded strangely muffled, breathless. A part of her yearned to throw her clothes off and jump on this hunk of man. She turned off the back burner, where the beans simmered.

Hank moved his hands down the slim curve of her hips.

Strange how he always seemed to know what she was thinking.

He tucked his big hands inside the legs of her cutoffs and up the sides of her hips, then pulled on the lower edge of her panties.

Sara arched against him, holding her breath.

He moved his hands to her waist and gently pushed it forward, bending her slightly over the stove.

Wow, was he going to take her right here, like this? He just might. She knew he was hard enough to. An erection the size of Hank's was difficult to hide. The way his cock felt, she knew she was in for a deliciously erotic adventure.

His hands went back up her hips.

Sara's core melted, an almost painful pull shooting through her groin. She pushed his hands down and turned to face him, wrapping her arms around his neck and kissing him. Taking his mouth with hers, she was a molten flood against his hard chest. Kissing him was electrifying.

He squeezed her against him, pressing his knee between hers. His hands moved to her ass and he pulled her into him with a groan.

She ran her hands through his hair, then gently pulled her mouth away from his. "Mmm." She sighed, looking up into his clear hazel eyes. "Are we getting ahead of ourselves?"

"I s'pose."

She grabbed a couple beers and led him to the sofa. Before things went any further, Sara wanted to level with him about her situation.

He pulled her down next to him, turned her sideways, and lifted her legs onto his lap.

This guy didn't waste any time, did he? But she had to admit she loved his quiet confidence. That was a big part of his sexiness. That energy of his.

Hank massaged her legs, running his hand down to the little white high heel ankle straps. "These shoes," he murmured, unbuckling the ankle straps. "I want you to wear them all the time…"

Sara raised her eyebrows at him.

He rubbed the delicate arch of her right foot, still in the shoe.

She rested her head against the sofa arm.

Hank slipped her high heel off and massaged her right foot, running his thumb firmly against the side of the arch.

Sara let out an ecstatic groan. "You sure know how to win a girl over," she murmured. "I adore having my feet touched!"

Again he rubbed the arch of her right foot with his thumb. Then he rubbed the whole foot with both hands.

His big, warm hands squeezing her foot sent liquid fire burning between her legs.

He slipped her high heel back on and ran one hand up her shin.

"Hank?"

"Mmm?"

"There's something I want to tell you."

"OK."

"I could use your help."

"You could?"

"I need to get out of town right away."

He studied her face, waiting for her to go on.

"Richard is trouble…"

"Right. I can tell that moron is trouble."

"No, really."

"What sort of trouble?"

She looked into those beautiful greenish eyes of his, yearning to tell him everything. But she couldn't bring herself to say the words. Tears sprang into her eyes.

"That's OK. I get it. No need for specifics."

"Thanks." She took a deep breath.

"Here's the deal, pretty lady." He gave her foot another squeeze. "I can get you out of town, and I'll teach you to drive my semi, but you'll have to go on a week-long run with me."

"Perfect!"

"Really?"

"Sure. Where you going?"

"San Diego, with a stop in Albuquerque."

"Wow."

"Around twenty-two hundred miles."

Sara could not believe her luck. She was finally going to hit the road, with a truly attractive trucker willing to teach her. Stupid Richard would have no idea where she'd gotten to.

"I have to leave in the morning," Hank was saying.

She took a sip of beer. "I can manage that."

"Great." He dug his thumb into her calf, just enough to release the muscle tension.

"Oh! That feels good."

"Lady, you have no idea…"

"No idea about what?"

"…how good I'm gonna make you feel." He rubbed her knee, pushing her legs slightly apart.

"Ah," she breathed. "That's what they all say, cowboy." She

grinned up at him.

"Some of us deliver." His warm hand moved up to stroke her inner thigh.

"I can only imagine." She shivered.

"You'll know soon enough." His voice was deep.

She tilted her head at him. "I do like a confident man."

"Good. Because…"

Sara waited.

"…there's a catch."

"A catch?" Her heart sank. Of course it was too good to be true. Nothing ever came that easily for her.

"A catch," he said, "a price." That hand of his moved a few more inches higher, rubbing her skin in small circles.

Again liquid fire shot through her groin. She held her breath and stared at him.

"In return for helping you, you will let me have my way with you."

She exhaled, looking down at her lap. Her cheeks were on fire. "Let you have your way with me," she repeated in a whisper. What the bloody hell did that mean?

"Yes," he said.

"What does that mean?"

"You have to trust me, Sara."

The way he said her name turned her on. It was a caress. But this was a shocking proposition. She didn't know him that well. What was he into? Did this amount to prostituting herself? On the other hand, she was just about to jump his bones anyway. What could be the harm? Maybe she was overdue for a week of wanton surrender. A sexual adventure. She could sure use an adventure. Especially a sexy one. She looked into his eyes again.

"I won't hurt you," he whispered, stroking her inner thigh even higher.

She squirmed, studying his face. It was a kind face. If his hand moved any higher, he would find out how crazily excited she was.

Hank's intense hazel eyes never left hers as he played with the lower edge of her panties.

Again she held her breath, mesmerized, unable to look away from him.

"I like a little bit of light kink, that's all."

Sara jerked her hips away from his fingers. "Oh, I don't know—"

He stopped her, putting the fingers of his other hand on her mouth.

She sat still, staring at him. She wished she knew exactly what sort of kinky shit he was into.

He'd found the inner edge of her panties again. "It's exciting," Hank told her, "intimate. It's about trusting, being vulnerable." He chose that moment to run his fingers inside her panties and lightly caress the folds of her lips.

Sara gasped, her eyes still locked on his.

He stroked more firmly, probing her slippery, sensitive folds, and pressed his fingertip against her wet gash.

He was so sexy, he took her breath away.

"Good," he said, penetrating her slick, hot private place with his finger. "I knew you were ready."

She swallowed, trying not to moan. It was as if his eyes were drilling into hers as he explored her. Sara had never wanted a man so badly. There was something about the way he touched her…something masterful and tender.

Hank slowly removed his finger and moved his hand back down her inner thigh, caressing and massaging her leg as he went. "We'll wait until we're on the road," he said in a tone of calm authority. "I need an answer, Sara."

"OK," she whispered. Had she completely lost her mind?

"OK what?"

"OK, I agree to your terms." What the hell was she agreeing to?

"Say it."

That sweet bossiness again. Thank God she was sitting, because her knees would have buckled. She took another deep breath and looked into his face again. "I agree to let you have your way with me, in return for taking me out of town and teaching me to drive your semi." Sara watched the corners of his sexy mouth turn up. Had she really just said that?

But she was cornered, she rationalized – desperate to escape Richard and to earn a decent living. Who knew what that wacked-out ex-husband of hers might do if he found her home? And she couldn't even go to work now. Plus, it might be fun to be Hank's submissive trucking whore. It was bound to be exciting.

"Good," he was saying. "Be sure to bring your swimsuit, lingerie, those high heels, and your pink waitress uniform."

"My waitress uniform?"

"Yep."

She looked up at him, confused.

"The way you look in that pink skirt turns me on, Sara."

CHAPTER 14

HANK

His belly full of Sara's tasty burritos, he cruised down the interstate to Cheyenne. He would have her soon, right here in the sleeper. He would leave her pink skirt and white high heels on, take her that way. He glanced around the dark cab and licked his lips. He was intensely drawn to her. It wasn't just a sex thing. It was… well, it was sexual, a physical thing. But it was also… everything. She was perfect. Just his type.

His mouth went dry. Maybe she was too perfect. Sara already mattered too much.

He hadn't been intimate with a woman since Becky. It was three years ago already. Becky. Hank groaned, remembering how sexy she'd been, willing to surrender to him. The two of them had fit together in every way. He was well aware that his needs were on the quirky side. The kinky side. Becky had loved his penchant for erotic spanking. Just sexy spanking. Light domination. Nothing heavy. It had made their sex so much hotter. His wife had loved it when he took charge. She'd always said it helped her relax and enjoy herself more.

Hank's heart ached, thinking of his lost love. His vision blurred from the tears in his eyes, and he knew he'd better think about something else. There was hardly any traffic tonight. When he got to Cheyenne, he'd stop somewhere for another beer.

In a way it was painful to date Sara. As much as he liked her – and he really, really liked her – the fact that she was not Becky hurt so bad it took his breath away.

But Sara was great. She even loved bald men! And she didn't care that he was older. He knew he turned her on.

He squinted in the headlights of the oncoming traffic. Some fool on the other side of the median refused to dim his brights. Hank hoped the idiot got a ticket. Seemed like the cops were never around when you needed 'em.

Yep, Sara was intensely drawn to him. He'd felt her heat tonight. Hank could have taken her right there and then. But he knew it would be better to let her anticipate being with him in the semi, far from home. He wanted the desire to build in her as she imagined what he meant by having his way with her. He was sure he had her mind flying like a sailboat in a gale.

He'd watched her closely when he offered her the bargain. Sara's eyes had darkened as her pupils dilated. Her nostrils had quivered, and she'd squirmed on the sofa. She was like Becky: she liked his bossiness. He knew what he was doing, and knew what he wanted. He knew what a sexy woman wanted, too. He knew Sara would lose that cool control of hers and come with him inside her.

The only thing Hank didn't know was whether or not he could get over Becky.

CHAPTER 15

SARA

She couldn't sleep. As Sara tossed and turned, she didn't know whether she was excited or just plain scared. I mean, her pink uniform skirt? Was he really insisting that she bring that along? Of course she would bring it. And wear it if he told her to.

She knew she would.

Sara lay on her back in the dark, imagining Hank as her teacher. In her waitress uniform, she would be a naughty tart. She'd tease him, slowly unbuttoning her top, opening it, pushing it down around her waist. Then she would undo the front clasps of her black bra and pull it open, holding her bare breasts with both hands. She would straddle his lap and give him a private dance.

Sara stroked herself. She was good at making herself come. In her mind, Hank held her waist as she did her lap dance for him. His big, callused hands explored her entire body. Suddenly he ripped her panties and took her, plunging his huge cock into her. Owning her.

Sara shuddered, writhing on her bed. "God!" she hollered, coming in an explosive burst.

***

Sara took Hank's offered hand and climbed into the Kenworth. She felt his intense gaze on her legs and knew he was pleased that she was wearing the waitress uniform. And the strappy high heels. She slid onto the passenger seat and tossed her duffle bag into the sleeper.

Hank hopped into his seat and off they went, southbound on Interstate 25.

"Sit here," he told her, patting the makeshift console he'd put between the two front seats.

Sara slid over and watched as he pointed out parts of the dashboard.

"Now I'm going to shift…watch carefully."

"OK." She leaned over and observed him working the gearshift, studying the timing of his movements.

"Now get on my lap."

"What?"

"On my lap."

"Now?"

"Yep."

"But—"

"Time for your first lesson."

She still hesitated, unsure of herself and him.

"We have a bargain."

Sara nodded. Her knees were weak and she was shaking all over.

"Come on."

Warily she moved onto his lap.

He positioned her between his arms as he steered the big rig down the interstate. "Get the feel of the wheel." He took her right hand and placed it on top of his right hand.

"Wow," she breathed.

"Now your other hand."

She did as he said. Sara could feel every movement and vibration of the wheel. And of his hands beneath hers. As he passed another semi, she gasped, feeling the way he steered.

After a few minutes, Hank moved his right hand, covering her hand with his. "Good." He murmured into her ear. "Now keep your hands where they are, y'hear?"

She nodded.

His right hand stroked the back of her hand and moved to her wrist and then to the tender skin of her inner arm. His thumb brushed her breast.

She jumped.

"What is it?" he asked. "You have gorgeous breasts." He touched her breast again.

She flinched.

"I forgot to ask you why you freaked out that night in Cheyenne…" Again he touched her breast.

This time she took her left hand off his and pushed his hand away. She put her left hand back on his immediately.

"Didn't I tell you to keep your hands on the wheel, Sara?" His voice was gruff.

"Yes, but—"

"But nothing. Answer my question."

She squirmed. "I don't want to talk about it." Her voice sounded strangled. She tried to slide off his lap.

But Hank held her in place, his right arm clamped tightly around her waist. "All right, I'll stop touching your lovely breast if you keep your hands on the wheel and relax into me."

As they crossed the Colorado state line, Sara managed to relax a little. She liked feeling his big, hairy hands as they roared down the road, and how his lean thighs moved under her as he worked the petals.

"His name was Johnny."

"Whose name was Johnny?"

"The guy who hurt me."

"Ah."

"He was the first man I opened up to after my divorce. He seemed great. But…"

Hank waited.

"I trusted him, but he freaked out over a scar I have on my left breast. I never heard from him again."

"Moron!"

"Yeah, I think so."

"Shit."

"He really hurt me."

"Damn…what kind of scar?"

Sara froze, unable to say anything.

"No matter," Hank finally murmured. "Listen to me. You're beautiful. I'm crazy about you. This Johnny must be an ignorant dickhead. A woman like you needs the real deal. I'm right here…" He bit her ear lobe, just hard enough to make her shiver.

***

Later that day, after stopping near Colorado Springs to grab some food and fuel up, he told Sara to get on his lap again. "Another lesson," he told her.

She sighed and crawled back onto his lap.

Instead of getting back on the interstate, Hank went under it.

"Where you going?"

"You'll see."

After a couple of miles, he pulled into a place with a dilapidated warehouse and a massive, empty parking lot.

"OK. You take the wheel."

"What?"

"Yes." He took his hands from the wheel.

She had no choice but to grab the wheel. Sara leaned forward, terrified but excited, and concentrated.

"Good," he said in her ear, moving his warm hands to her knees. He caressed her knees, then abruptly yanked her legs open and pulled her hips into him.

"NO!" She clutched at his arms, her ass pressed against his

hard heat.

"Don't we gave a deal?"

"Yes," she whispered. His jeans were rough against the tender skin of her inner thighs.

"Do you want me to teach you to drive this thing?"

"Yes…" Her voice was faint. She felt like she was going to swoon as he held her even tighter against him, his big hands on her inner thighs.

"Then keep your hands on the wheel!" Hank moved his hands higher.

She gulped, steering the semi around the vacant parking lot.

He ran his hands up and down her legs and played with the straps of her high heels. He tickled her shins and explored every inch of her legs, opening them wider.

Sara whimpered, feeling the tip of his swelling wood pressing harder against her ass.

He ran his hands under her skirt and pulled it up over her hips. Her feet dangling in the air on either side of his legs, Hank bunched the skirt up around her waist.

"What the hell?" she began.

"Hands on the wheel!"

"Oh my God! Hank!"

"Yes, my beauty?"

"I'm not… I can't…"

"What?"

Sara felt his hard cock against her wet heat. Soon he would discover how turned on she was.

"Mmmmm." He played with the lace edge of her panties.

"I will steer us into this wall!" The man was outrageous.

"No, you won't." He pressed the head of his cock against her cunt, which was still covered by the silky fabric of her panties. "You're steering just fine. Let's see what else you can do…"

Sara tried to squirm away from his cock.

He held her fast.

Oh my God, he was crazy sexy. She wanted him but felt helpless, with her hands on this damned steering wheel. One of his fingers slid inside the crotch of her panties.

She cried out.

"Ooh…" Hank lightly stroked her folds, pressing her ass against him harder.

Again she cried out.

"It's no use, my sweet." He ran his relentless finger up to her throbbing clit.

"No!"

"Don't say no to me," he growled in her ear.

Sara shuddered helplessly. Never in her life had she felt such electricity. But he still hadn't seen the breast cancer scar, she thought.

"Keep steering." Hank shifted her to the right, so she was pressed against his right thigh, and pushed her panties down just enough to bare her ass. He held one hand firmly on her sex and stroked her ass with his other hand. He gave her a casual spank, low on her ass.

Sara jumped. "Hey!"

"That made you hotter and wetter."

"No…" she whispered.

"I told you not to say no to me." He spanked her again, harder.

Again she jumped. Horrified by being turned on by it, she whimpered.

"I love your sweet ass." He pushed her panties down and took them off one of her legs. He left them dangling from one of her ankles, just above the ankle strap of her high heels. "I like how that looks." He ran his hands back up her legs, pushing her knees open again.

Overwhelmed, she had to concentrate on steering. She couldn't believe he was doing this.

His finger touched her clit.

She jumped.

"So sensitive." He gave her clit a gentle pinch.

"Hank!"

"I like hearing you holler my name," he murmured in her ear.

"Please…"

"Please what, sexy lady? All right." He pressed two of his fingers into her.

"Oh!"

"Nice and tight. You liked those little spanks, didn't you?"

Again she tried to squirm.

"Answer me," he growled.

"Yes," she said in a small voice.

"Yes what, naughty girl?"

"Yes, I liked those little spanks."

"Good. Cuz I liked 'em too." Again he pressed the tip of his hard cock against her sex. With one hand he unbuttoned the top of her uniform.

"Oh no!" She tensed up, cringing.

"What are you worried about?" He opened her top and pushed it off her shoulders. Running his hands under her bra, he shoved it up and held her by both breasts.

She wanted to pull away from him but couldn't.

"I have you right where I want you, babe."

Sara was totally at his mercy – trapped by having to keep her hands on the wheel, his stiff cock poised for action, her legs wide open, her bare feet dangling in the air as the big rig bounced. Any time he wanted to, he could plunge into her.

He played with her nipples, pinching them gently. He caressed both of her breasts.

She arched against him involuntarily.

He felt the scar on the outside of her left breast. Rubbing it, he asked her what it was.

"My scar," she said, her heart hammering.

"From what?"

"Breast cancer."

"Oh. God damned cancer." He rubbed the scar gently. "Pull over."

She did. Now what?

He took it out of gear, letting it idle. "I want to look."

"Oh, come on…"

"Show me," he said, turning her sideways on his lap.

Mortified, she let him look.

Hank kissed the scar. "It's beautiful, just like you."

Tears sprang into Sara's eyes and she melted into him, her hands on his chest as she kissed him.

He played with her left breast, stroking the scar. His other hand was on her clit again.

"Oh my God!" She squirmed.

"Steer." He grabbed one of her knees and pushed it open, spreading her legs even wider now, his legs between hers and his erection pushing insistently against her. He put the semi in gear, forcing her to steer again. "I want to show you something, sweet Sara."

"What?" she whispered.

"I'm gonna show you that you're sexier than ever. Fuck that cancer shit."

Was he going to fuck her while making her steer? But she was relaxing into it now. He loved her body, scar and all. She should have told him long ago.

"Dance for me."

"What?"

"Dance for me." He pinched her clit.

She jumped, jerking her pelvis.

"That's it."

"Oooh…" She had to keep the damned truck away from that warehouse.

Hank massaged her clit and pinched it again

Groaning, Sara arched.

"Yes!" He pushed his hard cock into her slippery cunt, holding her knees open. "Oh Sara…"

"Oh my God!" Again she arched her back. She couldn't help it.

"Steer!"

There was nothing to do but steer, helpless, as he rocked her, sliding the length of his beautiful cock in and out of her slowly. He still held her clit. "God!" This was so crazy. But she loved it. Hank was big but not too big. Just right for rocking and plunging. "It feels so good," she whispered, "it's been so long…"

"I want you."

"Oooooohhh…"

"Now park this thing."

She steered to the edge of the lot. "Oh God," she moaned as he slid his cock deeper into her.

"Good girl. Turn it off."

She did.

Hank lifted her from his lap and took her to the sleeper. He stood behind her, pushed her knees open with his knees, and bent her over the bed. "Mmm, those high heels make you just the right height, babe." He ran his stiff cock up and down her crack, and rammed her slippery cunt.

Sara groaned.

"I've wanted you like this since the first day I saw you…" Again he bunched her pink skirt up around her waist. He pushed her waist down and fucked her deeper.

She couldn't get enough of him! Now Sara knew: they really were "fuck me" shoes. Standing in her high heels, her ass was nice and high as he plunged all the way into her from behind.

His hot groin slapped against her as he fucked her hard. She felt like she was dissolving somehow, melting into him. He pushed her skirt higher around her waist, and pressed her waist down harder, making her ass stick up higher as he slammed into her. One of his big hands was spreading her ass, the other playing with her crack.

She felt something press on her ass hole. "No," she whimpered, squirming.

"I love it when you squirm, Sara." He pushed his finger on her tight anus.

"Ooh I don't know about this," she panted, "I've never done this…" But oh my God he felt good, filling her up just right, not too big. The wild motion, his sweet rocking rhythm, the way he touched her, owned her. It was astonishing, captivating. He was mounting her and fucking her like an animal, but the way he did it was loving and tender and oh God, so sexy! He made her feel like a real, whole woman, a desirable, sexy woman. She'd been craving this.

He gave her a sharp spank.

Sara gasped.

"Mmmmmm," He rubbed her clit as his rod impaled her hot center.

She came almost instantly.

So did he, exploding inside her.

"GOD!" They hollered in unison.

He stayed inside her, lightly running his fingers up and down her back. He eased them both onto the bed and wrapped his arms around her from behind.

Sara snuggled in Hank's arms, holding one of his hands. She loved the feeling of his arms around her. The man had just taken her to new heights. It was dizzying. Sara'd thought this part of her life was over for good. She loved Hank's unapologetic, raw sexuality. His confidence. She'd never known it was even possible to orgasm the way she just had with him. It was as if a buried part of her was coming to life in his hands, from his kisses, from his stiff cock deep inside her.

She was his.

CHAPTER 16

HANK

He woke up when Sara moved away from him. Hank lay behind her, his arm resting on her hip. Her skirt was still bunched around her waist. Sunshine slanted through the sleeper skylight.

She pulled her skirt down.

"No," he muttered sleepily, pulling it back up.

She turned and looked at him.

He pushed her skirt higher. "I think you have the sexiest ass I've ever seen, Sara."

"Have you seen a lot of them?" Sara cocked her head at him, lifting her eyebrows.

He sat up, moved back so he could lean against the wall, and pulled her onto his lap, facing him. He gently cupped her breasts, looking at her scar. "Tell me more about this."

Sara sighed. "It was three years ago. Could have been much worse. Early stage, low grade. But … I don't know. I feel damaged." She turned her face away.

He kissed her nipples.

"Must you?" she whispered.

"Must I what?"

"Play with my breasts. I told you…"

"We have a deal, lady."

She gazed at him, her wide gray eyes shining.

"I mean to see that you keep your end of the bargain." He

71

wondered if those were tears in her eyes. "I won't hurt you, Sara."

She was silent.

"I might fuck your brains out, but I will NOT hurt you." He held her small wrists behind her with one big hand, and she arched involuntarily. He liked how her breasts looked when she arched. His cock was leaping back to life already. He kissed her nipples again, pulling on each one with his lips.

She shuddered.

Hank moved his mouth to her scar and began kissing it.

Sara gasped.

Hank licked the brown scar, and ran his tongue around it, then kissed it again.

She moaned.

"You have gorgeous breasts." With his free hand he played with her nipples.

She held her breath.

Hank massaged her stiff scar, studying it at close range.

She squirmed uncomfortably.

He caressed the scar. "That guy, the moron…what was his name?"

"Johnny," she said breathily.

"He must be a total idiot. You're beautiful." Hank kissed a smaller, higher scar. "What's this?"

"That's where they took out a lymph node."

Tears sprang into Hank's eyes.

"What is it?"

"I lost my wife Becky to cancer. Lung cancer."

"Oh, God. I'm so sorry!" Sara nuzzled his cheek with her nose. It felt cool against his skin.

"Am I going to lose you, too?" he blurted, immediately wanting to kick himself for saying it.

"What? No way! The only place I'm going is with you on the road, Hank Werner."

"I like hearing you say my name." He kissed her scar again,

ran his fingers over it lightly, and stroked her all over.

"Oh, you do, do you, Hank Werner?"

"Yes, I do, Sara Cooke." He held her chin, forcing her to look him in the eye. "Your radiation scar is a battle scar of a victorious warrior. You're here, sweetie, and you're one of the sexiest women I've EVER met!" He lightly caressed her sharp cheekbone and touched her nose affectionately.

She had tears in her eyes again.

He took her mouth, slowly kissing her as he played with one nipple.

She groaned and whimpered, arching her back.

Hank ran his lips down her throat, along her collar bone, and back up to her jawline. He took her mouth again, more urgently. He could not get enough of this woman. How did she manage to be shy and slightly modest, yet at the same time wildly sexy? Something about her turned his crank in a crazy way. He was gonna fuck her till the cows came home. He'd teach her new pleasures she'd never imagined. Then he'd bang her some more.

When he let go of her wrists, she ran her hands through his salt-and-pepper hair. With her fingers she lightly touched his shoulders, his arms, his chest, his belly, his back.

Hank tenderly kissed the brown scar again. Somehow Sara was melting his frozen, grief-stricken icicle of a heart. He'd been shut off for so long. Again he ran his tongue around the scar, moving his hands to that gorgeous ass of hers.

"Um...Don't we need to get some driving done?" She grinned down at him.

"We'll make it up later..." He watched her close her eyes as he massaged her ass. He felt her juices flowing and his rod stiffened against her heat. He rubbed the head of his phallus along her slippery entrance. He didn't mean to rush things, but she drove him crazy.

She shuddered and wrapped her arms around his neck. "Oh, babe..." she whispered.

He slid his cock into her, filling her slowly.

Sara rode him gently, sweetly, her cunt slick and hot and tight. Smooth.

They kissed and kissed, Hank handling her ass as she rode him. He spread her cheeks and explored her ass with his fingers.

Again Sara gasped.

He pushed his finger against her anus.

She moaned, but kissed him more deeply.

He fucked her harder.

She rocked her hips back and forth on his cock and his finger entered her ass.

"Oh my God!" she panted. "Oh my God!"

Hank drove his finger further into her. Not too far, just a little bit.

"GOD!" she screamed.

He sucked her nipples, teasing them with his teeth, his finger penetrating her ass as they bucked.

She rocked and shuddered as she came. "HANK!"

Hank loved feeling her fiery flood, and came deep inside her. "SARA!"

They wilted together, happily winded, and held each other tight.

As the day's light faded, Sara still straddled his lap, her face nestled against his neck.

CHAPTER 17

SARA

When she awakened, the sleeper was dark except for one low light over the miniature kitchen sink. Hank put something in the microwave and that light came on, too. Sara curled up on her side under the thin blanket and sniffed the air. Probably cheese. She was starving. How long had she been asleep? And how long had it been since she'd eaten? Under the blanket she was half naked, her skirt still up around her waist. She stretched. How shameless could she get? But she had to admit she loved it. All of it. She felt sore between her legs. She blushed to herself, remembering how she'd gotten sore. Wow. She may be out of practice, but she was happy to get "back in the saddle" with a man like Hank.

She tucked the blanket under her chin and silently watched him make sandwiches. The sleeper was amazingly comfortable. The bed was better than any RV bed she'd ever seen. The little blinds on the side windows were closed.

"Good morning, Sleeping Beauty," Hank said.

"Mmmm, is it really morning?"

He shook his head, grinning at her.

"Something smells good."

"Let's eat!" Hank set up a little table between the bed and

the passenger seat, which was swiveled around to face the bed. He put plates of sandwiches on it and grabbed sodas from the tiny fridge beneath the sink. It was the most compact kitchen Sara'd ever seen. He took two bowls from the microwave, set them on the table, and sat in the passenger seat.

Whatever was steaming in the bowls smelled divine. She straightened her clothes and scooted to the edge of the bed, wrapping the blanket around her like a shawl. "This looks great, Hank. I'm starving!"

"I'm not surprised," he replied with a wink.

Sara chuckled. "Mac and cheese, my favorite!" She blew on it. "How did you know?"

"Dumb luck," Hank said, his mouth full of ham sandwich.

The mac and cheese was burning hot, so she dove into her sandwich. It was delicious, with just the right amount of mustard. She and Hank were even compatible with food, she thought, amazed. "That was quite a first lesson, cowboy," she teased.

He reached across and tugged on her hair. "We haven't even begun, woman!"

She gazed into his eyes, turning serious. "I thought my life was over."

"Me too."

The low light caught the hollow beneath his cheekbones. He was one heckuva good-looking guy. Sara's penchant for good-looking men had gotten her into trouble in the past. Her mind flashed to Richard and what she'd promised him. What the hell would happen when she got home? What would Hank think if he knew what she's promised that ex of hers? Should she tell him? She should.

"Penny for your thoughts."

"Hmm?" Sara felt dreamy, being in this semi with Hank.

"Where'd you go?"

She touched his cheek. "Just stupid worries." She'd tell him soon. Not right now. It was so peaceful and cozy having supper with him in here. There'd be plenty of time to worry about that stuff later. She had a week, after all. Looking around the cab, Sara felt a thrill. She'd waited so long for this. So far she was not disappointed.

Watching Hank eat, she couldn't help but wonder what his next "lesson" would entail.

CHAPTER 18

HANK

"The funniest one is my last name, Werner," he said, watching Sara drive the semi around the rest area parking lot, her bare arms tan in the rosy sunset.

"What do you mean?"

"When truckers say it, it means "We Employ Rookies, No Experience Required."

"Wow! That's quite a code."

"Truckers have their own language, especially on the radio."

"I've noticed," she replied. "I have no idea what they're talking about on there."

"Next time I'm driving, you can use my laptop and go to a web site about trucker lingo."

"Great."

"They have a long list. You won't believe it." She seemed like a natural, with a good feel for handling the eighteen-wheeler. Hank was pleased with her progress, but knew she needed practice shifting. That would come on the road. It had been a long day, and the delivery stop in Albuquerque had slowed them down considerably. They were now back on schedule. Hank hated to rush through southern New Mexico and miss bathing in his favorite desert hot springs. He'd make sure they came back through here on the way home.

He rolled his window down. The blue-gray clouds gathering on the horizon were rimmed in gold from the sunset. It was hot and surprisingly humid. Distant thunder rumbled and lightning flashed in the dark clouds. The air was heavy with electricity. He watched the muscles of Sara's brown legs as she worked the pedals in her sexy black tank top and short cutoffs. The stringy fringe of the denim shorts was bright white against her long, tan legs. Those legs…Hank's manhood again sprang to stiff attention, like a soldier eager for action. He shifted to ease the strain of his cock swelling against his jeans. Well, what the hell, he hadn't bothered her all day. The perfect chance for another lesson.

"Pull over, ok?"

She steered into a parking spot and stopped.

"Keep your hand on the stick."

She did.

He covered her hand with his.

Sara glanced over at him.

"Turn the engine off."

She did.

"Let's take a break."

"OK."

Huge raindrops began pelting the semi as he led her to the bed, where they sat. He hand-fed her a juicy peach they'd bought at a farm stand a while ago. The rain drummed against the sleeper roof.

She kicked off her sandals.

"Put those high heels on, babe."

She raised her eyebrows at him, but did as he said.

Hank licked peach juice from her chin and wrapped Sara in his arms as he ran his tongue up to her mouth. He flicked his tongue into her soft, sweet lips and took her mouth. He pulled her onto his lap, facing him, kissed her again, and slid his hands inside her tank top, running his fingers up and down her back. Lifting her top over her head, he tossed it into a corner.

When he held and kissed her breasts, she moaned softly and

arched against him, her lips curving into a seductive smile. She leaned back and unbuttoned her cutoffs.

Hank played with her high heel straps and ran his hand into her shorts. She was all liquid fire.

"Oh!" she cried when he tickled her clit.

His other hand traced the curve of her hip as he breathed in her incredible scent of lime and herbs. Telling himself to slow the hell down, he reached over and grabbed another peach. He couldn't take his hand off her crease. She had an addictive sweetness to her. He took a bite of the peach and fed her some, then dripped it on her breasts. He licked the juice off and kissed her nipples, gently biting one of them.

"Ooh." She squirmed.

It was too much. He took his hand from her cutoffs. "Come on," he said, standing up. He climbed onto the bed and pulled her with him. The rain pounded on the roof as he lay her out on the mattress and opened a window.

"Wow, it's pouring," she said.

"Sure is." The scent of wet dirt and fragrant Creosote shrubs wafted in. He fixed his gaze on her as he unzipped his jeans.

Her eyes widened.

He rolled onto her, his legs pushing hers apart as he pinned her beneath him. Hank grabbed her knees, lifted them high, and propped her legs on his shoulders. He loved how she looked, her high heels up next to his ears. He yanked her open cutoffs and panties down, stroked her mound once with his pulsing cock, and plunged straight and deep into the heart of her.

"OH!"

The shocked surprise on Sara's face spurred him on. He'd caught her off guard, getting right to it. He would teach her that she was his – anytime, anywhere. Hank didn't have to look at her flushed face to know she wanted him. He knew from the heat in her slick canal as he stroked all the way in and almost all the way out, going deep. God, she was beautiful, her brown hair splayed out on the pillow beneath her head.

"You sure don't waste time, do you?" she murmured.

"Damned right, babe." He drove into her harder.

She tried to take off her cutoffs.

"No, leave 'em." His jeans were still on as he fucked her deeper yet. Damn, she felt good! He loved how she couldn't move in this position, except to thrust up against his plunging. He had the control, her high heels thrown over his shoulders. "I've got you where I want you."

She moaned in rhythm with his thrusts, holding his upper arms tighter and tighter. Her fingernails cut into his skin. Sara didn't seem to mind her helplessness in this position. God, he loved her for that. She was wetter and hotter. And that hair. She was fucking gorgeous. She could take all of his length. She wasn't afraid or in pain. She was tight and wet and hot and long. Perfect! He thrust and thrust, watching her face as he rubbed the arch of her sexy foot. He ran his hand up the side of her leg and stroked her sweet ass, bracing himself with his other hand and pushing her legs higher with his body. Thrusting deeper, he touched her anus.

"No," she whispered.

"Don't say no to me," he growled, ramming her and giving her a swift spank.

She cooed, rubbing his hair with both of her hands. "Yes, sir," she murmured so faintly he wasn't sure if he'd heard her right.

He put his finger back on her tight hole, pressing harder.

She bucked, using her calves on his shoulders for leverage. "GOD!" she screamed, shuddering as she came.

"AAH!" He exploded deep in her.

"My God!" she whispered, trying to move.

Hank held her fast, staying inside her. He had a feeling he'd get hard again right away.

He was right.

"You're a machine." She smiled that slow, sexy grin of hers.

"A fucking, loving machine." He grabbed one of her high

heels and moved it to his other shoulder. Now both of her legs were on his right shoulder. "OK, you can take 'em off," he told her.

Sara slowly wiggled out of her cutoffs, her clear gray eyes fixed on his.

It felt good when she moved like that with him inside her. He watched her bedroom eyes – sleepy, sexy, wild. Ready for anything. He thrust a little.

"Oh!" She pulled her lavender panties off her ankles, then tossed them into the corner.

"Yes." He caressed her curvy ass and gave her another sharp spank.

She jerked, surprised.

He spanked her again.

"Ow! That hurts…"

"Good." He delivered another smack to her lower ass.

"Why?" she pleaded.

"You need it, my sweet. You need it bad." As he rubbed her ass and spanked her again, her molten juices flowed around his cock, buried deep in her cunt.

She peeled off his T-shirt, tossed it in a corner, and ran her hands along his arms, shoulders, back, neck, and face.

He took one of her fingers into his mouth and sucked it. "You're so beautiful, Sara," he whispered when he released her finger, "like the desert rain."

"Mmm." She tried to pull his jeans down his legs.

"No. I want to stay inside you."

She stopped.

Already the spanking was working, he thought as he took her mouth. He grabbed her foot by the high heel strap and moved it back to his other shoulder, so she had one leg on each of his shoulders. He thrust a little to see how hard he was. Getting there. He tickled the outside of her thighs, the backs of her knees, her feet, and her groin.

She jumped and giggled, ticklish.

He played with her ass again.

"You sure do like my ass."

"You have no idea, babe," he said, his tone threatening yet sweet. He pulled one of her feet closer. Holding it by her open toe stiletto, as he licked the tip of her big toe.

She gasped, caressing his shoulders.

He sucked her toes, one at a time, slowly, then kissed her calf. He ran his fingers lightly up her ankle, inside her calf, and up her inner thigh. She was going to find out what it meant to be fucked slowly, for hours. "I love having you right where I want you, woman."

"Mmm, Hank," she sighed.

"On your back, helpless." He pressed her legs higher with his weight and rubbed her butthole with his index finger.

She bucked. "NO!"

Man, it was good when she bucked like that. "Don't say no to me." He spanked her and pushed his finger against that sensitive hole.

"But…"

"Yes."

She squirmed.

"Squirm all you like, babe. Feels good." He tried thrusting again. Almost ready. He pushed his finger a bit harder on her anus.

When Sara squirmed again, his finger entered her. "Oh my God!" she blurted.

He worked his finger further into her ass, rubbing the skin between her anus and her crease with his thumb.

She bucked.

His thumb rubbed harder. He pushed his finger deeper into her ass.

She was writhing. "Oh my God! Oh my God!"

With his thumb he pressed the skin between her cunt and her anus.

She tried to kick.

"Naughty girl," he muttered, grabbing her ankle. "That will cost you." He held her ankle firmly with one hand. Removing his other hand from her ass, he plunged straight into her cunt, deeper than before. This position was so good for going deep.

Sara gasped, shuddering.

"How much can you take, babe?"

"I can take it all." She moaned low in her throat, her lips swollen and dark from his kisses.

"Say it, Sara."

She looked at him. "Fuck me," she whispered so faintly he almost couldn't hear her.

"Louder."

"Fuck me!" she whimpered.

He bucked, stroking her tan legs and holding her gorgeous ass with both hands as his full weight on her pushed her legs higher on his shoulders. When he took her mouth, it sent her legs even higher and his thrusts went deeper. He rammed her for all he was worth, squeezing her ass cheeks and spanking her.

She flinched.

But Hank saw that her eyes were dilating madly, so he spanked her a little more. Her love juice flowed hotter and thicker around his rod. Oh, she liked being spanked all right.

"CHRIST!" she yelled, shuddering and writhing as she came.

"BABE!" Hank felt like he was detonating deep inside her. He saw stars.

CHAPTER 19

SARA

She shifted and smiled to herself. Driving the huge rig felt natural to her. Sara had thought it would be difficult to move through all the gears, but it wasn't bad. Not bad at all. She had a lot to learn about the CB radio trucker lingo, but that would come with time. Being on the road was even better than she'd imagined: the wide open desert stretched out in front of her, under a deep blue sky.

Sara loved this powerful, smooth Kenworth. So far Hank had her driving on secondary highways only. It was great, though. For some reason it reminded her of the first time she'd ridden her mother's big horse. Sara'd been eight years old that day.

The minute she was finished with this stint of driving, she'd call her daughter. And Annie. She couldn't wait to tell them about driving the semi, and learning trucker lingo. They were probably worried about her.

Sara felt like her whole world was opening up in front of her eyes, as wide open as this clear, high desert sky. It was as if her nerves were on fire, she felt so alive. She would try to describe all of this to Lexie and Annie – well, not the censored, private parts of the trip. She smiled to herself again.

**

Hank held her hand under the table, tickling her palm with his finger. The southern New Mexico sunshine streamed through the truck stop's big windows as the waitress brought their orders of Huevos Rancheros. Hank said this Las Cruces truck stop had the best breakfasts in the west. As usual he knew the waitress, a pretty young thing named Jill.

Sara had to admit that she felt a twinge of jealousy as Hank laughed with this Jill. She sighed, hating herself for her jealousy or insecurity or whatever the hell this was. Damn! Why couldn't she ever play it cool? Why did she always wind up in emotional knots when she got sexually involved with a man? What was her problem?

"Something wrong?" Hank nudged her shoulder with his.

"No. Why?"

"That was one heckuva big sigh."

"I guess I'm a little tired."

"Gee, I wonder why." He gave her a lewd wink.

Sara grinned at him and dug into her food. It was scrumptious, with homemade salsa between layers of eggs, refried beans, and tortillas. "Mmmm," she said. "You're right, this is the best." She watched Hank wolf his down. The two of them had again worked up impressive appetites. What a trip, she thought. Eating and screwing their way across the Desert Southwest.

"Best in the West," he said.

"They have showers here, right?"

"Yep." He held up the shower kit he'd brought.

"It's gonna feel so good to take a shower!"

"Sure will." He leaned in close. "I'm dragging you into the shower with me, hot mama," he whispered in her ear.

Sara shivered, her core on fire again from his words. What was it about the way he said things, the way he handled her, the way he took charge? She could not get enough of Hank Werner.

***

She let the nozzle blast her back as she soaped up Hank's scrub rag. How long had it been since she'd had a shower? Sara had no idea. She had lost track of how many days they'd been on the road. Who cared? She was having the time of her life. It was especially sweet since she'd given up hope on ever finding love again.

Hank stepped into the stall and wrapped his arms around her.

They kissed, letting the hot water soak their hair. Curls of steam rose around them.

Sara scrubbed his back with the soapy scrub rag.

"Mmm," he hummed happily, turning his back to her.

She finished soaping him up and began scrubbing herself.

"Oh no, you don't," he said, grabbing the rag from her. He soaped it up again and washed her from head to toe, even shampooing her hair. It was divine when he scrubbed her scalp with his fingernails. She wondered how much hot water this place had.

Hank stood behind her as he soaped up the rag again. Then he dropped the bar of soap. It landed in front of Sara's feet.

"Pick it up, would you, babe?"

She hesitated. "Yeah, right!" She'd heard plenty of bawdy jokes about dropping the soap in the shower.

"Don't we have a deal, sexy mama?" He ran his hands down her belly.

Her knees almost buckled. She leaned back against him, turning her head. "Are you a maniac or what?"

"Absolutely."

She made a show of it, arching and writhing from his touch, then bending way over to pick up the damned soap.

Hank held her hips and thrust straight into her from behind, not even opening her legs.

"Oh!" she yelped, surprised again. He got so hard so fast. The man knew what he wanted, and he went for it.

"Quiet," he commanded, pushing her waist down and opening her knees with his as he impaled her wet, hot center.

"What?" She tried to twist around and look at him, and he

gave her a light spank.

"People will hear you," he told her. "Thin walls."

"Mmmph," she groaned with her mouth closed as he positioned himself to go deeper yet, pressing her knees open and grinding against her mound. His cock was perfectly curved for this. Sara had never realized it could feel so good from behind. It must be the shape of Hank's cock. As it stroked her G-spot again and again, she moaned and whimpered, trying not to make much noise.

It wasn't easy.

He plunged into her hard and her head almost hit the shower faucet. "Oh, babe," he crooned, both of his big hands on her ass as he fucked her harder. "You drive me crazy!"

"Oooh Hank!" she whispered, rocking her slender hips against him in rhythm with his frenzied thrusts. He spread her ass cheeks, touching her anus again. This time her knees really did buckle.

He held her hips and eased them both to their knees.

"God!" she whispered, resting her elbows on the floor as he bent her over again. God, he was sexy!

Hank boned her for all he was worth, smacking her ass now and then.

When he pressed his finger on her anus, Sara whimpered, holding her hand over her mouth. "Mmmph! GOD!"

"JESUS!" he hissed as he came deep inside her.

"OOOH!" She held her hand over her mouth as she spasmed with her own powerful eruption.

***

Even though they'd had coffee and it was early, they almost dozed off again as they snuggled in the sleeper. This wild sex was wiping her out, Sara thought, but had there ever been a more delicious exhaustion? She'd never felt anything like this.

Certainly not with Richard.

Of all the times to think of friggin' Richard. Sara shook her head at herself. The Richard dilemma – it had been worrying her, in the back of her mind. Hanging over her like the dread of overdue homework. But she hadn't told Hank.

Her eyes flew open and she sat up. "There's something I have to tell you."

He propped himself on one elbow, his big Tom-Selleck-bedroom eyes sleepy. "Shoot."

"Remember I said Richard is trouble?"

He nodded.

"One night he came over. I shouldn't have answered the door but I did, and he pushed his way in."

Hank raised his eyebrows.

"He was mean drunk. I thought he was going to rape me…"

He stroked her arm, his face grim.

"Then I remembered how much he used to hate it when I had my period…"

He waited.

"…so I told him I had my period…and…"

"And?"

"I acted like I wanted to have sex with him…"

"And?"

"I promised to have sex with him when my period was finished."

"You didn't think it was important to tell me this sooner?"

Sara stared at his tense face. His mouth was a thin line now.

"Didn't you promise to be totally honest with me?"

"Yes." She gulped. "I'm sorry! I was afraid to tell you—"

"You are a very naughty girl, Sara," he interrupted, his voice stern.

Meeting his eyes, she detected a glint of laughter there. "It's not funny!" How dare he laugh at her!

"I know." He stroked her forearm again, lightly,

Hank's fingernails tickled her arm, making her shiver. "I had to get him out of my house!" She covered her face.

He put his arms around her. "I understand."

"Do you?" she asked, fighting tears. Sara hated how she tended to cry when she wanted to be strong. She took a deep breath, trying to get it together.

"Yes." Hank was deadly calm.

"He was going to rape me that night."

"I'm gonna kick his ass!"

Sara took another deep, shuddering breath, then lowered her hands from her face. "I got a restraining order."

"Good!"

She nodded. "But Richard is going to be really angry…"

"I'm sure he will be."

"He is dangerous, Hank. Probably always has been. But he's way worse now."

He nodded. "Listen, we'll figure this out. I can protect you from that creep. You will NEVER honor that promise to Richard – in fact, you had better NOT honor it."

"But he knows where I live—"

"Sara," he interrupted again, "I won't let you be home alone."

"Good!" She blew her nose as gracefully as she could. "My hero," she cooed, relieved to have finally told him. She wrapped her arms around his neck and planted a sweet kiss on his sexy lips.

Hank kissed her back vigorously, his tongue tasting her mouth.

His hands were on her hair as she melted into the kiss, her center once again blazing. Were they going to have sex yet again?

Hank stroked her ass. "No way is your ex getting any of this," he growled, slipping his hand inside her shorts.

Sara held her breath. The man's touch drove her wilder and wilder.

"He had his chance and he blew it," he was saying. "If he gets anywhere near you, he'll regret the day he was born."

A fierce swell of love flooded her. She wanted to tell Hank that she loved him. She couldn't say the words. Her mouth was clamped shut. Hell, it was probably too soon to say it anyway, she figured. Was there anything worse than saying that too soon, and not having it reciprocated?

He moved his hand to her waist, then gave her ass a sharp slap.

She jumped, widening her eyes at him.

"That's for keeping a secret from me." He spanked her again.

Sara hated to admit how his big hand smacking her ass fueled the inferno between her legs.

"Promise you'll always be completely honest with me."

"I promise," she whispered, ready to give him anything.

"Never be afraid to tell me the truth, Sara."

"OK," she whispered, running one finger along his cheekbone.

"I'm going to punish you…"

"What?"

"…for keeping that secret."

"But—"

"But nothing. Think about your punishment."

She swallowed.

"Not right now. We have to cover some ground."

"Right."

"You drive."

"On the interstate? You sure I'm ready?"

"You're always ready," he said in his deep, sexy voice.

***

"Were you naughty to keep that secret from me?"

"Yes…" Sara whispered, her cheeks aflame.

Hank sat on the edge of the bed. "Take off your shorts."

She did.

He pulled her over his knee and held her waist down. Her bare feet dangled in the air. Hank ran his hand inside the top band and bared her ass.

She steeled herself for the spanks she thought were coming, then gasped as his hand moved down between her legs, rubbing her inner thighs as he pushed the lacy panties down to her knees.

Sara tried to squeeze her legs together, but was bent far over his lap. She was sure he had a good view of her juicy slit anyway.

Slowly he ran his big hand back up her inner thighs, pushing them slightly open. Up he went until he reached her most sensitive skin. He jammed two fingers into her cunt.

She groaned.

"Nice." He thrust his fingers all the way into her.

Sara squirmed and groaned again.

"BE STILL," he told her.

She whimpered again.

"QUIET."

She tried to look at him, but couldn't.

He rubbed her ass and delivered a hard smack on her left cheek.

She jerked, but was silent.

Smack! Hank spanked her lower ass again.

She whimpered, but very quietly this time.

Smack! A harder spank landed on that same spot.

"Ouch!" She squirmed. "No…"

"I told you not to say no to me, babe." Smack! "I like how pink your ass is, Sara." Hank stroked her ass cheeks and caressed her ass crack.

God! What was he going to do?

He spanked her a couple more times. "Sara?"

"Yes?" she responded, her voice weak.

"I want you to have a safe word."

"A safe word?"

"A word you can say if you need me to stop."

"Oh."

"The best word is 'red,' for stop."

"OK."

"You are only to use it if you seriously cannot handle what I'm doing."

"OK," she whispered, shivering again as he stroked her ass possessively.

"Now I'm going to spank you ten more times."

She held her breath.

He held her waist down and paddled her in earnest, one smack after another, low on her ass.

It stung, but Sara managed to muffle her cries. But by the tenth spank she couldn't help but kick her legs.

He rubbed her sore ass and ran his fingers into her cunt again, massaging her clit with his thumb.

"Oh!" she cried.

Hank held her over his knees, driving her crazy by running his fingers up and down her crease.

She was hotter than she'd ever been, ready for him to throw her on the bed and fuck her hard.

Instead Sara felt his fingertip pushing into her tight ass hole.

She squirmed helplessly. "Please, Hank, no!"

"I won't hurt you," he said gently as he pushed his finger against her anus again.

"Please no..." she pleaded, fighting tears again.

"Do we have a bargain?"

She nodded silently.

"Sara," he said, "what is our agreement?" He pushed a little further into her anus.

"Oh! That you can have your way..."

"Say the whole thing."

"That you would get me out of Chugwater and teach me to drive your semi if I let you have your way with me." She shivered, feeling his damned finger pushing harder.

"Good," he said. "You're going to learn what that means, my sweet."

CHAPTER 20
HANK

He would introduce Sara to his erotic toys, one by one. Hank had a whole bag of them, stowed in the back of a cupboard. He hadn't used them since losing Becky. In fact, he'd begun to wonder if he would ever use them again.

He would give her merciless pleasure, he thought, sipping his beer and gazing at her as she sat on the bed watching one of the late night TV shows.

"What?" she asked him.

"Hmmm." He took out his bag of toys.

"What's that?"

"You'll see."

He lay down next to her and stripped off her clothes.

She looked at him, a question in her wide-set eyes.

Her body was beautiful, the sleeper's low lights throwing deep shadows across her. Hank strapped the vibrator to his hand and ran his vibrating palm along her shoulder, down and up her arm, and cupped her breast.

Sara arched exquisitely when he touched her nipple with his vibrating fingers. "Wow," she whispered.

"You've never seen one of these?" he asked her.

She shook her head, arching again as he stroked her other nipple.

Hank cradled her as he massaged her belly and her legs. He turned her over and rubbed her back, making her groan. Carefully avoiding her ass, he massaged the backs of her legs and her feet.

He used one of her slim ankles to turn her back over. God, she was gorgeous. Sara was so relaxed, she felt like putty in his hands. He took both of her wrists in his other hand and held them above her head, running his vibrating palm along her knees and up her inner thighs. He opened her legs as he massaged her, barely brushing her mound with the side of his hand. Finally he reached her wet heat.

She gasped from the intensity, writhing as he rubbed her cleft.

He focused on her clit with his vibrating hand, rubbing it in quick circles. He took her mouth as she shuddered with her orgasm, muffling her cries with his kiss.

Hank thrust his vibrating fingers into her cunt.

"Oooh," she crooned.

He brought her to the brink, then teased her sensitive clitoris again.

Sara bucked on the bed, trying to free her wrists.

Hank held them fast in his strong hand.

"God!" she panted as she came again.

Merciless, he kept his vibrating palm on her clit.

She thrashed, her face twisting as if she was in pain.

"You OK, Sara?" he asked, not letting up on her clit.

"It hurts," she whimpered, wriggling.

"It hurts good, though?"

She nodded, squirming and bucking her lovely hips.

Hank loved watching her. She came again and again, helpless against his intense touch on her clit.

He released her wrists, turned off the vibrator, and took it off his hand.

Sara lay there, spent. "Wicked man," she whispered.

He put her limp arms around his neck and took her sensuous

mouth again.

"What about you?" she murmured when she came up for air.

"I'll wait."

CHAPTER 21

SARA

She couldn't help but wonder. Hank was so masterful at turning her on to sensations she'd never felt before, he must have tons of experience. Where had he learned all this?

She tried to keep her questions to herself.

She really tried.

But then they stopped at yet another truck stop where he knew the damned waitress – too well, Sara felt.

She waited until they were back on the interstate.

"Hank," she began, taking a deep breath, "I have to ask you something."

"OK."

"You're amazing in bed…"

"Thanks."

"You're so good, you must do these things all the time, right? With lots of women?"

"No." He said it simply, in a hushed tone.

She looked at him. "But where did you learn--"

"No," he cut her off, staring at the road ahead.

***

She lay on her side in the dark and felt him stiffening behind her. Sara straightened her bottom leg and bent her top leg toward her chest, resting it on the bed.

Hank wasted no time entering her, resting his legs behind hers and wrapping his arm around her. It was slow and intimate as he held her tight, thrusting rhythmically. Hank gently kissed her neck and ears, his rhythm building.

"Unnh!" he moaned.

She was surprised how quickly he came.

He rolled her onto her back and held up a curved cucumber.

"What the hell?" She had no idea what he was up to. But knowing him, she was sure it would be fun.

He lay on his side and caressed her thighs with the cucumber, opening them. Soon he was rubbing it up and down her slit.

Her center was red-hot.

Hank thrust the cucumber into her.

"Oh!" she yelled, surprised at how it felt. It was different, mostly because of the curved shape.

He fucked her with it, watching as if in a trance.

The tip was hitting her G-spot. Sara felt the pressure building and took a deep breath, needing to push down hard. She held her breath and exploded in a new and different way. "God!" she cried. It felt wonderful, the best she'd ever had. As it subsided, she felt depleted. She couldn't even get up to deal with the fact that the bed under her was wet.

Hank rolled her onto some dry blankets, and covered both of them with the comforter.

"Did I pee when I came?" she asked sheepishly.

"No, that's G-spot fluid," he whispered in her ear. "It's sweet, like you are, sexy mama."

***

In the blue-purple dusk, Sara sank into the hot water. It felt silky and wonderful on her skin. They were somewhere in southern California. She found herself so immersed in Hank, she didn't even know where she was. She would have to work on that if she aimed to become a professional driver.

But not right now.

On one edge of the desert hot spring, a warm waterfall tumbled into the creek below.

Beside her, Hank took off his trunks and lay back in the water, gazing at the sky. He reached over, untied her bikini strings, and tossed her suit onto the rocks at the edge of the pool.

"Hey!" she protested.

"Hey what?" He ran his hands up and down her silky back, then took her hand and placed it on his cock.

"Hey, you're a maniac!" She stroked his amazingly stiff rod, looking around to make sure no one was around. At least they'd be concealed by the dark.

"Guilty…" Hank thrust a little against her hand. He got up and sat on the edge of the pool, leaving her seated at his feet.

Sara kissed his knees and thighs, moving her mouth to his impressive staff. His hands were in her hair as she gently licked and kissed his manhood, shyly sucked the tip, tentatively ran her tongue under that rim, and sucked again.

"Sweet," he moaned, rocking his hips slightly.

Sara wanted to please him.

He groaned, his big hands cradling her skull as she sucked. Lifting her head, he slid back into the pool and took her mouth. Then he lifted her so that she sat on the edge of the pool. He pushed her knees open, running his hot mouth up one inner thigh.

"What if someone sees?" She covered her breasts.

"Fuck 'em," he muttered, moving his lips closer to her center.

"Hank!" she hissed, wanting to holler but not wishing to attract attention. He was so outrageous!

He ignored her, his big hands on her ass as he licked the junction of her thighs.

Sara jerked as his mouth reached her entrance and tickled her most sensitive area. "Hank!" she whispered again.

He ran his hot tongue into her canal.

"Oooh," she whimpered, writhing. She could feel his teeth on her clit!

He ran his teeth gently but firmly on her bud.

Sara gasped, panting. He drove her crazy!

He slid her back into the water, wrapped her legs around his waist, and took her mouth.

Then he plunged straight into her.

Her scream was muffled by their kiss.

Hank pulled almost all the way out and thrust deep again.

Sara whimpered in ecstasy, trying not to make any noise. She loved how he taught her new things, brought her new experiences. If he wasn't so bossy, she would never have had the courage to have sex outdoors like this. He was different from anyone she'd known. She thanked God for him.

He stood in the pool, held her ass, again wrapped her legs around his waist, and ground into her.

She held on for dear life as he penetrated the very heart of her.

The waterfall was pounding on his back as he fucked her even deeper.

Shuddering, she lay back in the hot water, droplets from the waterfall sprinkling her face. Her ears submerged, she stretched her arms above her head, her hair floating in the water. "Oooh," she whimpered as his rod hit her G-spot, gazing at the inky-blue sky. Were the stars real, or was she seeing stars from this divine feeling of surrender. She hadn't known she craved surrender. But she did. She really did. This was what she'd been wanting all her life—

Hank abruptly pulled her up as he sank into the water.

"What the—?"

"Someone's out there." He peered into the dark desert.

CHAPTER 22

HANK

As it turned out, the only intruders near the hot spring were a doe and fawn wandering through the nighttime cactus. Hank smiled to himself. He and Sara had had no trouble finishing what they'd started in the pool.

God, did she turn his crank!

In the dark cab he watched her handle the thick southern California traffic like a pro as they cruised through the San Diego suburbs. After their soak, she'd thrown on her long green robe. He happened to know she was wearing absolutely nothing under that robe.

Normally that would have driven him wild, but Hank was spent – for now anyway. He had to admit that he was satisfied at the moment. For once. The angles of Sara's face glowed in the headlights of the oncoming traffic. She was keeping the semi steady as cars zipped around them like pesky flies.

Soon he would take over. It looked like a bad traffic night. Sara's enthusiasm for driving the Kenworth had them ahead of schedule. Hank could count on one hand how many times that had happened to him. He smiled to himself again. He'd find a Wally World where they could park for the night. After unloading tomorrow they could take the whole day off. He wanted to take Sara to his favorite beach out on Coronado Island.

***

She laughed, running ahead of him down the Silver Strand beach. She sprinted into the shallow water and kicked salt water at him. She knew damned well he hated getting his jeans wet. The minx! She would get hers. At least he'd taken his cowboy boots off in the semi. He trotted up to drier sand and flopped down. They'd been out here for hours, walking, talking, lying in the sun, looking for shells. They'd found moon snail shells, cockle shells, and sand dollars.

He leaned back on his hands and watched Sara skip in the knee-deep ocean, the late sun sparkling on the ocean behind her. He'd known she would love this beach. Silver Strand was on a sand-spit, on the outer edge of San Diego Bay. The sweeping, white ocean beach was two and a half miles long. There was another half-mile of beach on the bay side. He'd always meant to camp here, but never had time. He would have to do something about that. The park had a campground right on the sand, good fishing, and plenty of barbecue pits.

This was what Hank loved about being a trucker. How many folks could live in southeastern Wyoming and still get to this San Diego beach often? How many knew the best cafes and hot springs in the West?

He gazed at Sara's dancing silhouette, the windblown surf behind her backlit by the low sun. God, it was beautiful. She was beautiful. He felt a tug on his heart as he studied her. And the familiar tug in his groin. His stomach growled. How long had it been since they'd eaten? He couldn't even remember. He'd make hamburgers with all the trimmings.

Now she was loping toward him, flapping her arms like a bird. "Woooohoooo!" she hollered, twirling.

He grinned at her as she sank onto the sand next to him.

"I can see why this is your favorite beach, Hank!"

"Yep, gotta love it."

"I feel great!"

"Me too!"

"What is it about a beach?" She opened her arms as if to embrace the sea.

"It'd be great to camp here."

"That would be fantastic!"

"I'm ready for some grub, are you?" Hank's stomach growled again.

"Come to think of it, I am."

"I want hamburgers."

"Perfect."

"And beer and tequila shots."

"Mmmm."

"Cribbage!"

"Sure, it's fun beating your pants off at crib." She laughed.

It was true. She'd beat him every time so far. "Nope," he told her. "I'm gonna skunk you good."

***

This was what it was all about, he thought, watching Sara in the golden glow of sunset. She leaned on her elbows at the little table where Hank's antler crib board was center stage. In her faded jeans and yellow T-shirt, she was already brown from their day at the beach.

They'd each won one game. This third game would be the tie-breaker. He would be the real winner this evening, he thought, studying her as he sipped his drink. He'd cut himself off after this one. Any more booze and he wouldn't be in top form for the real fun. Just thinking about it, he felt pressure in his groin.

She was in for it this time.

Waiting for her to play, Hank leaned back in the swiveled passenger seat and gazed at the scarlet-rimmed clouds. The ocean breeze wafted in the open windows along with the roar of the pounding surf.

His need had been building all day and now he felt the heat of the tequila in his belly. Hank was in the mood for more – the perfect state of mind for delivering the punishment he'd promised her. He would push her this time.

She was tipsy, which would help her relax. He wanted her to enjoy what he had planned. It was what he and Becky had had together. It was what he wanted from his woman.

"I'm out!" Sara crowed, moving her pin to the finish line. "Gotcha again," she added, giggling.

"Yes you did." He grinned at her, stroking her forearm with his thumb. "You're gonna pay for that, Miss Sexy."

"Ooooh, I'm scared-a youuu," she teased, tossing her hair.

He smiled again, packing up the crib set. He stashed the crib board in a cupboard and took out the plaid bag. His toys. He took a deep breath, closed the windows, and pulled the mini-blinds. In the quickly fading light, he lit a jar candle and set it on the table. "Put on your waitress outfit," he told her. "And the high heels."

She rolled her eyes.

"You're gonna pay for that, too, young lady."

She tossed her hair again and finished her drink. Sitting on the edge of the bed, she slowly peeled off her jeans and T-shirt.

He gazed at her lavender panties as she wiggled the skirt down over her slim hips, put the shirt on, and buttoned it.

She leaned down to slip her brown feet into the delicate white high heels. Giggling again, Sara stood up and staggered a little. She tucked her shirt in.

"Come here." He patted the bed next to him.

She did.

"Lie back."

"What are you—"

"Shhh." He put his right pointing finger on her curvy lips.

Sara gazed into his eyes.

He kissed her, deeply, insistently, holding her head in his

hands.

"Mmmm," she groaned.

"Lie back," he said again.

This time she didn't question him.

Hank lay on his side next to her, regarding her as he ran his fingers down the length of her pink uniform. He lightly tickled her legs, running his fingers all the way down to her thin ankle strap and bare toes. He rubbed the high arch of her pretty foot.

Sara seemed mesmerized.

He took one of his vibrators from the bag and strapped it on the back of his right hand. Tickling her thighs, he moved his vibrating hand up under her skirt and touched the heat between her legs.

Sara inhaled sharply.

Through the silky fabric of her panties, he could feel her steamy, slippery crease. He left her uniform on as he massaged her belly and breasts, arms, and neck. Kissing her again, he ran his vibrating hand inside her shirt and on her nipples.

"Ooh," she sighed, writhing, "that feels so good..."

Sara was putty in his hands. He rolled her over, pulled her shirt up, and massaged her upper back and shoulders and neck.

"Mmm," she moaned.

He slowly moved down her back, pressing his vibrating fingers into her muscles. Lower and lower he went. He pushed the skirt up and rubbed her muscular ass, making her squirm. Hank deliberately ran his vibrating hand on the backs of her thighs, along her inner thighs, up and down, pushing her legs open a little. He massaged her cleft again, through her lavender panties, then slipped his vibrating fingers inside her panties and straight into her pulsating, wet slit.

"Ooh," she crooned. "You trying to drive me crazy?"

"Absolutely," he told her, moving to her clit.

She jumped. "God!"

He slid his finger to her anus. It was like playing a violin, he thought, holding his vibrating finger against her tightest hole.

"Oh! No…" Sara tried to move away from his insistent finger.

"Don't say no to me," he said in a deadly calm voice.

"What?" She sounded like she was in a daze.

"Don't say no to me."

She tried to turn over.

He held her fast with one hand, the other busy fingering her tight hole.

"Oooh." She squirmed. "Fuck me," she whispered faintly.

"Yes," he growled.

He smiled, enjoying how she looked writhing on his bed, her pink skirt pushed up to her sweet little waist. Oh, he would fuck her all right. Just not the way she had in mind. He emptied the bag onto the bed. He would make sure it didn't hurt. He would take his time, be patient, and use plenty of lube.

She hiccuped.

"Did you have too much to drink?"

She giggled. "I think so."

"Naughty girl." He took the vibrator off his hand, tossed it in the corner, and pulled her over his lap so that her exquisite ass was in the air.

She laughed. "Yes, so naughty." She hiccuped again.

He pushed her waist down and spanked her lightly, through her panties.

"Oooh!" she teased, as if playing a part.

Hank stroked the backs of her thighs and looked at her shapely, lavender-clad rear end. She had the sexiest bottom he'd ever seen! He delivered a couple of gentle spanks over her lace-edged panties, then tucked his hand under the bottom lace edge. He pulled the panties down a little.

She jerked and hiccuped again, giggling at herself.

"Are you a bad girl, Sara?"

"No."

"ARE YOU A BAD GIRL?" He held that bottom lace edge and pulled down her panties, baring her smooth, creamy ass. He loved how she looked with her panties pulled down just enough, like this.

"Maybe…" she whispered, quivering. She hiccuped again.

"Are you a bad girl?" Hank asked again.

"Yes," she whispered.

He slid his fingers between her legs and rubbed her clit.

Sara panted, wiggling.

"Count out the twenty spanks I'm going to give you."

"Twenty?" She gulped.

"Yes," he replied, delivering the first smack on her lower ass.

She jumped. "One…"

He slapped her ass again.

"Two…"

Hank loved watching her ass shake and vibrate as he turned it red with his hand. Smack! Smack!

"Four," she whispered.

He rubbed her bottom and caressed her wet lady lips. They were swollen, inviting. Smack! Smack!

"Six…"

He slid his hand to her clit and played with her.

Sara bucked from his touch.

He gave her a series of quick, sharp spanks.

She bucked again. "Ow," she groaned. "Eleven."

Again he rubbed her ass and stroked her wet heat.

Another series of stinging spanks had her begging him to stop. "Seventeen," she moaned, trying to reach back to protect her bare butt from him.

"Three more," he said, holding her wrists behind her waist with one hand. He aimed the last three very low, just above her thighs, to warm her up even more.

"…twenty," she whimpered as he stroked her hot, red ass.

After a minute, she began to get up.

"Not so fast, my dear." Hank put a generous blob of Vaseline on his index finger and rubbed it on her anus.

"Not that!"

"Sshhh."

"Spanking's not enough?"

"No," he told her. "I want what I want." He slowly, carefully worked his slippery finger into her tight hole. His cock leaped, eager to fuck her.

Sara quivered and moaned. "I'm afraid…"

"Trust me." He let go of her wrists, rubbed her red ass cheeks, and moved his finger a little deeper.

She panted.

"Stay still, my sweet." He removed his finger and cleaned it. He picked up the blue silicone butt plug, put Vaseline on it, and pressed the narrow tip against her anus, pushing slowly.

Sara bucked, trying to twist around.

He held her waist down firmly.

"What is that?" she cried.

"My favorite toy." Hank pushed it in further. He loved watching the shiny silicone plug sliding into her tight virgin anus, its cone shape stretching her.

Sara writhed. "I've never done this…"

"I know, my sweet." He penetrated her further with the plug, its wider middle stretching her tight orifice.

She panted.

"Relax, my love."

"I can't, I don't know," she whispered.

Hank held the end of the plug, pushing it in and out a little. He slowly, patiently penetrated her, watching the flared base of the plug get closer to her anus. He loved how the flared base looked moving up and down as he played with Sara's sexy ass. He loved her curves. "Oh, babe, I love your ass!" he said. "It was the first thing I noticed about you…"

She whimpered.

"The plug is designed for this, babe. It can stay there as long as I want it to." He pushed again, harder this time.

When Sara bucked, it made the plug go deeper into her.

"RELAX, my love."

"Please..." she pleaded. "No..."

"What did you say?"

"No..."

"Didn't I tell you not to say no to me?"

"Yes."

He gave her a swift, light spank, aiming it to push the plug into her.

She jerked and kicked her legs. "Oh my God!"

Hank knew that the toy's flared base would keep it from going too far into her. He spanked her again, lightly.

"Ohhh!" Again she tried to cover her ass with her hands.

Again he grabbed her wrists. He stroked her cleft. She was wetter and hotter than ever. She did like it! He teased her little bud.

She gasped, sobbing a little.

"Sara..."

Silence.

"Sara!"

"Yes?" She whispered in a faint voice.

"I'm going to fuck your ass with my big cock."

"God!"

He lightly ran his fingernails on her ass and slid her lacy panties down her legs. He slowly moved his hand back up the insides of her legs, parting them slightly.

She moaned.

Picking up his green, curved dildo, he slid it into her dripping cunt.

"Oohhhh," she sighed.

Hank pulled the dildo partway out, watching the wetness on it. He thrust it back into her.

"Ohhhh!"

He spanked her lightly again, very low, so that the spanks pushed the dildo deep into her.

"My God!"

He pushed the dildo and the plug into her at the same time.

"Ooohhhhhhhhhhhhhhhh!"

He rolled Sara onto her side and stood at the edge of the bed.

"What the…?" she began.

He rolled her onto her stomach and bent her over the bed.

"You're so sexy, my love!" Hank lifted her hips and slid his favorite wedge pillow under her. The pillow lifted her ass into a perfect position for deep penetration. God, he loved how she looked: erotic, trusting, wanton, her slender hips pressed against the edge of the bed, the pink skirt pushed up around her waist. She would be braced against the bed now. Leaving the butt plug in, he slid the dildo from her hot depths and thrust his throbbing cock into her. God, she was beautiful!

"Oh, Hank…"

He pushed her waist down, spread her knees open with his knees, and speared her with forceful plunges that made his balls slap against her. He moved his hands to her ass, spreading her cheeks and fucking her even deeper.

"Ooh!" Sara cried in rhythm with the long strokes of his hard cock.

He stopped and pulled the plug out, which made her jerk. He rubbed more lube on her anus, lubed his cock, and pressed it against her tight hole.

"Oh no, oh, God," she moaned.

"Don't be afraid, my love."

"But…"

"Trust me."

She was quiet.

Again he pressed his firm member against her ass, this time penetrating a little.

She gasped.

"Rub your clit, Sara."

She moaned.

"Rub your clit for me, babe."

She reached down and began stroking her clit.

"Good, babe." He felt her muscle tense. "Open up to me, Sara..."

"I can't..." she whispered.

He pushed a little harder.

She jerked, gasping again. "No," she whispered.

"Don't say no to me, Sara."

She whimpered, rubbing her clitoris.

Hank had never seen such a sexy woman. "Let me in, babe. I want your ass." He pushed his cock harder against her anus.

"It hurts!" Sara cried. "Wait a minute..." She was panting, almost sobbing.

"Open for me." He waited, holding his cock still but making sure not to pull out. He wasn't about to give up. He held his penis where it was, insistent, hard, demanding her surrender.

After a few moments she relaxed and let him into her beautiful, tight chamber.

"Good girl," he growled, stroking her ass cheeks as he gently, carefully entered her anus.

She opened more.

"Good girl," he repeated, pulling his rod almost all the way out, putting more Vaseline on it, and pushing it deeper into her ass.

"Ooh!"

"Does that hurt, babe?"

"No," she answered, sounding amazed.

"Good girl!"

She relaxed her muscles, letting him in further.

He loved this. He loved knowing that Sara had opened herself to him. He loved that it was her first time this way. He loved revealing her hidden desires. He moved slowly but insistently. Hank loved watching her, bent over his bed. He knew she must be very turned on, to relax like this and let him in. There was something about entering a woman's ass that was so extremely hot. It was the surrender. It was the way she had to give herself to him mentally, to submit, to yield control. It was the tight resistance of her anus, the way she gripped the bed with white knuckles. The way she arched her back and threw her head up, her hair stuck to her sweaty back. The way she began to push back slightly. The way she moaned now, a guttural, deep sound. "Ready for me to fuck your ass, Sara?"

"I don't know," she whispered.

He thrust a little, spreading her cheeks with his hands.

"I don't know…" she whimpered.

He added more Vaseline. "Say it," he told her.

"What?"

"You know."

"Fuck me," she whispered.

"Louder, babe."

"Fuck me!"

"Where do you want me to fuck you, Sara?"

"My ass."

"Say it."

"Fuck my ass," she moaned.

Hank plunged into her.

She seemed to hold her breath, but was still relaxed.

Her anus was slick and tight, so good. "Sara…" he managed to say. "I'm fucking your ass!"

She moaned again, trembling.

Hank poured a different lube on his staff.

"Oh, babe," she sobbed.

"You OK?"

Sara rocked her hips in answer.

"How much can you take?"

She pushed against him.

What a woman! He thrust into her ass in earnest.

She bucked a little.

She was his. All his. He would find her g-spot from here, toward the front of her sleek, sweaty body.

"Oh my God!" Sara hollered, bucking again.

He'd found and hit that perfect spot. He held her cheeks wide, pinning her against the edge of the bed, and impaled her again and again, for all he was worth. He'd been waiting forever for this.

"GOD!!" Sara screamed, her body spasming from the power of her huge orgasm.

"Jesus!" Hank hollered as he let himself go, filling her ass with his hot cream.

CHAPTER 23
SARA

She had no idea why she began sobbing right after that great orgasm. She was trembling, too.

Hank leaned forward and stroked her back. He kissed her shoulders and neck, and the side of her face.

"Don't look at me," she said between sobs. She hated it when people saw her cry.

"Baby, baby," he crooned.

Sara could not stop weeping. She was spent. She wished she understood why she was crying. Probably overwhelmed. Overwhelmed by how owned she felt, how satisfied she was. This was a part of her she'd never known existed. Her, a submissive woman? But she had to admit that part of her was willing to hand over the controls to her man.

She'd heard about erotic spanking. Lots of people found it a real turn-on. But she'd never thought that applied to her. The way Hank took charge, helping himself to her, owning her in a loving way. The way he paced himself between pleasure and pain. The way he insisted on her submission. The way he breathed, moved, fucked, talked. The way he was opening her up to a whole new world of erotic pleasure.

Everything.

It was so different.

She was falling in love. That was it! She was in love with Hank, and it scared the crap out of her. He had never spoken of love. Was it just too soon? Or was he a player?

Sara hadn't loved anyone for a long, long time.

She imagined jumping up, getting dressed, gathering her things, and getting the hell out of here.

"Come here," Hank murmured, gathering her in his arms.

"Don't look at me!" she wailed, turning her head away.

He lay her on the bed.

She rolled away, facing the wall, and curled into the fetal position.

Hank cuddled her from behind, spooning her, his strong arm around her waist. "You OK?"

She nodded, unable to speak.

He slid his bottom arm under her neck. "I know it's intense, especially the first time," he murmured.

Sara nodded again. She had no words.

Enveloped in his arms, she took deep breaths. Slowly she drifted into a deep sleep.

***

"Did you roll your eyes at me?" Hank turned in the passenger seat.

Sara shrugged, hungry and tired. She'd been driving the semi all day. They were almost in Tucson already.

"Take the next exit, and go into the truck stop parking lot."

She did.

"Away from the others."

She glanced at his unsmiling face and knew she was in for it. In spite of herself, her body responded with wet heat between her legs. "I'm really hungry."

He gazed out the windshield.

"Can we eat first?"

"Nope."

"But—"

"But nothing." He grabbed her hand and pulled her out of the driver seat. Sitting on the edge of the bed, he heaved her over his knee and delivered five sharp spanks on her denim-covered behind.

Sara kicked her legs.

Hank smacked her bare legs, held them down, and slid his other hand up under her cut-offs.

She squirmed.

"Get up," he told her.

"What?"

"Get up!"

Stunned, Sara stood.

"Take off your cut-offs."

"But I—"

He glanced at his watch. "The more disobedient you are, Sara, the more discipline I will give you."

"Discipline."

"Yes."

She pressed her knees together, standing next to him, all too aware of her body's reaction to his threat. Between her legs, she was a quivering mass of hot jelly. She didn't want him to feel that. But what could she do? Slowly she unbuttoned her cut-offs. She slid them down her legs, stepped out of them, and kicked them to the side.

Hank pulled her over his knee again, smacking her panty-clad rear end.

Again she kicked her legs.

He smacked her legs again, grabbing one of her inner thighs.

"Oh!" she gasped.

Hank slid his fingers into her panties, caressing her slick heat.

She bucked, hoping he would plunge his fingers into her. He was teasing her so lightly, she could barely feel his fingers.

He pulled her panties down abruptly, just far enough to bare her bottom. Holding her waist, he spanked her lower ass, one cheek and then the other.

It was beginning to really sting. "Ow!" she cried, squirming to get away.

He spanked her two more times, hard.

"Ow!" She tried to cover her ass with her hands.

"Quiet. Hands on the bed."

Sara paused, then obeyed. She clutched the bedspread, fisting her hands as if hanging on for dear life.

Hank opened a cupboard door.

She couldn't see what he was doing.

He rubbed her ass and gave her another spank. He stroked her vulva with the hard tip of something, spreading her swollen, sensitive lips with it. "Mmmm, sexy. Too bad."

"Too bad?"

He gave her a spank.

She jerked from the surprising impact of it.

"Yes," he said, stroking her clit with that tip thing.

Sara jerked again.

"Too bad you need discipline now, not pleasure. How I would love to give us both pleasure. How I would love to fuck your beautiful, hot, wet cunt."

Sara moaned, wanting him more than she'd ever wanted anything.

Hank ran the tip back down her gash, and pressed it against her anus.

She jumped, throwing her head up.

He pushed the tip into her ass.

She tried to kick her legs, but he held her fast. The butt plug. It had to be.

He pushed it into her ass, as deep as he could.

Sara moaned.

"Quiet!" he ordered, lightly spanking her so that he hit the plug.

Sara jumped from the impact.

"I won't make you wear the plug while we have dinner," he told her, rubbing her sore, hot cheeks.

"Thank you," she whispered.

"If you continue to be disobedient or disrespectful, you'll wear the plug."

Sara was silent.

"Do you understand?"

She nodded mutely.

He spanked her three more times.

She sobbed.

"Are you going to be good?"

"Yes," she whimpered.

He rubbed her ass again, and caressed her pulsating, slippery cleft. "Your body is beautiful."

She loved being over his knee, her ass his. "You're beautiful, too," she managed to say.

"Thank you, Sara."

When Hank took the plug from her ass, Sara stifled her moan. She twitched her hips as he fingered her lady lips again, hoping he would give in and give her a good, hard fucking. She wanted his hard cock. She wanted it now! How could a spanking turn her on like this? She'd never felt so hot.

Hank stroked her clit. "You are gorgeously fuckable, my Sara."

She rocked her hips in time to his strokes.

He tapped her vulva with a light smack, making her jump. "I need to eat, so you must wait."

"OK," she murmured faintly.

He pushed her further over his knee, sending her ass higher into the air. "After we eat, I will give you a good fucking, if you behave well during dinner."

"OK," she whispered.

"You are not allowed to pleasure yourself, Sara."

She didn't know what to say. How would he even know if she did?

"For dinner you will wear the skirt, with no underwear." He pulled her panties all the way off her legs and threw them on the bed.

Sara whimpered. "But…"

"You need more spanking?" he asked, his big hand on her ass.

"No."

"No what?"

"No, sir."

***

Under the table, Hank held the inside of her knee. He fed her a French fry and inched his hand up her leg.

Sara tried to act as if she wasn't sitting here bare-assed under a skirt. Good God! At least they were sitting in a corner by themselves. The crazy thing was, she liked feeling owned by Hank. Sara felt as if she were awakening for the first time, sexually. She would never have thought she would like being dominated. Maybe it was just him. He knew exactly what he was doing.

He fed her another fry and licked the salt off her lips.

Sara swooned inside, swept in a wave of adoration. She could not believe it. She might even get religion, since God had sent him to her. She'd earned it, though, with the miserable men she'd let into her life.

Hank. His need to dominate fit with her apparent need to submit. It was strangely relaxing, having him in charge. It left Sara free to relax and enjoy the pleasure – and even the pain. She could stop him with the safe word. That was key to the whole thing. She trusted him.

Hank's warm hand moved up her inner thigh, possessive and confident, pushing her legs slightly open.

No wonder he'd picked a booth in an empty section, far from the other truck stop customers, she thought, squirming.

"I love it when you squirm," he crooned in her ear.

Sara took a bite of her salad. This whole thing was so intense. Hank was wild and kinky, yet tender, careful, and patient. He was more loving than any man she'd ever known. The way he'd cuddled her last night was so intimate. They spooned all night.

As intense as the pleasure was, it was triggering intense feelings in her. She couldn't help it. It was that line between pleasure and pain, the closeness between a dominant and his submissive.

The waitress walked up to the table and Hank quickly moved his hand back to her knee.

Sara glanced at him. Had he just winked at the waitress? Did he know the damned waitress, again? This one was older, with salt-and-pepper hair in a single braid. Sara excused herself to go to the ladies' room.

When she came out, Hank and the waitress were talking.

They abruptly stopped when Sara sat down.

The waitress cleared their plates.

Instantly Sara wanted to bolt. That fast, she was so uncomfortable her skin was crawling. She wasn't cut out for emotional roller coaster rides. She could swear that waitress was flirting with him. Sara was raw. Vulnerable somehow. Why didn't he explain?

He sat there, his hat pulled down over his forehead as he sipped his black coffee.

Hank didn't put his hand back on her leg. She gritted her teeth. Something had shifted, but what? The whole time they'd been on this trip, she'd tried hard not to worry about what would happen when they got home. The more she fell for Hank, the more difficult it was not to worry. He was addictive. What if he dumped her? What if he was just using her?

She sat up straighter, telling herself to stop with the damned what-ifs. They never got anyone anywhere. Her life would be better because of this trip, no matter what. She would have her CDL. No more waitressing. She must keep her focus on that.

Easier said than done, though.

Sara had to admit that she wanted him to be part of her life forever. What was he feeling? She couldn't read him. As open as he was with her sexually, he was all clammed up about his feelings. Typical man.

It was her own fault. She always fell for the strong, silent cowboy type. There was a huge downside to that: an utter lack of communication.

***

As promised, he gave her a wonderful fucking after dinner. It was great. The best. She'd exploded in multiple orgasms, straddling Hank's lap, his hands and cock driving her crazy. She'd never had multiple orgasms in her life.

It was so good, Sara felt even worse. Somehow the better the sex was, the more she had to lose. Why was it that whenever she got sexually involved, she ended up with anxiety? She lay there on her back in the dark, her heart pounding as she watched the stars through the skylight. It was a beautiful, clear desert night.

Next to her, Hank was still. His breathing was even and steady.

Sara felt like there was a hopelessly dense wall between them.

She'd finally asked him who the waitress was.

"Nobody," he'd replied.

Sara had left it at that, determined not to be one of those naggy women. She would keep her fears to herself. Now she wondered if she could get up, pack her things, and leave without waking him up.

It was mighty tempting. She could hitchhike home from here, no problem. She should get away while the getting was good.

Protect herself. She couldn't handle feeling so vulnerable with someone who would not communicate. She couldn't handle any more of his feral sex that had her falling for him. It had her gaga like a silly schoolgirl. She couldn't handle her mind racing, her heart pounding like this, her insecurities rearing up like raging mustang stallions.

She'd give it one more day. That was it. She'd see what happened tomorrow.

CHAPTER 24

HANK

He shifted and turned the wipers to high, cruising through one of those southern Arizona gully-washers. The rig hydroplaned and he slowed down. Hank wanted to make it to Truth or Consequences, New Mexico, to his favorite hot springs. The one on the Rio Grande. Glancing over at her, Hank smiled. She sure was sleeping a lot today. Maybe he was wearing her out. He grinned again. No way. Not her. He'd meant to help her out and give her some pleasure. But he had to admit it: He was falling for her. In spite of himself. In spite of hanging on to Becky. Hank knew damned good and well that Becky would want him to move on. She would want him to enjoy his life.

With Sara he would enjoy his life all right. They were such a good fit and, man, had he been right about her ass. She had an ass that just didn't quit. And she loved being pulled over his knee…

He was pretty sure she was falling for him, too. Not that she'd said anything. Not yet. They had plenty of time for all that. He liked the idea of them being trucking partners, crisscrossing Wyoming and the West, having wild sex whenever they felt like it.

It was time to level with her about Charlie. But he wasn't ready to talk about all that. Not with anyone.

CHAPTER 25
RICHARD

He guzzled the rest of his beer, wondering again where the hell his ex had gotten to. Damn. She'd promised him a good screw. Richard looked around the log bar and squinted. Crap. He was seeing double again. He waved to the bartender. "Hey!" he hollered.

"Hay is for horses," the bar man told him. "You're cut off."

"What?"

"You. Cut off."

"Bullshit!"

"This guy giving you trouble, Alex?" someone said.

"You could call it that," the bartender replied.

Richard wheeled around. "You!" It was the son-of-a-bitch who'd broken his nose. "I'm gonna beat the crap outa you."

"You haven't learned a damned thing, have you?" the man asked him.

This guy had a way of getting under his skin. Just pissed him off. Richard threw a drunken punch. Problem was, he missed.

Richard never saw it coming.

The guy's beefy fist slammed into his nose with a sickening crunch, re-breaking it.

"Fuck!" Richard howled, crumpling to the floor. He held his bleeding nose, rolling around in pain. "Motherfucker!"

The guy and his buddies dragged Richard to their pickup and

threw him in the backseat of the king cab.

"Ow!" Richard wailed.

"Shut the fuck up," the big guy growled.

One of them gave Richard a paper towel for his bloody nose. "Try not to shit yourself, you worthless piece of garbage," he muttered.

"Lemme outa here!" Richard tried to open the door.

The big guy leaned in and poked Richard in the chest, hard. "If you don't sit there and shut up," he snarled, "I'm gonna kill ya."

Seemed like the guy meant it. Richard leaned against the corner, holding the paper towel under his bloody nose. Christ, it hurt!

One of them got in the driver seat, and off they went. The truck had a rough ride.

Richard felt every bump in his nose.

They pulled over and parked in the sagebrush.

"Maybe this time you'll learn something, dickhead," the big guy said, dragging him out of the pickup and sitting him against a skinny tree. "This is for you to find when you're sober," he added, pinning a note on Richard's shirt. "It says stay the hell out of Chugwater or else. Got it?"

"Got it," Richard slurred, pretending to salute.

The truck spun out in the gravel, did a U-turn, and headed back to town.

Richard watched the taillights disappear into the black night. Then he passed out.

CHAPTER 26

SARA

She cradled her cell phone on her shoulder. Sitting at the counter while Hank fueled up the semi, Sara's jaw dropped.

"They re-broke his nose and dumped his drunken butt out in the sagebrush, and told him to stay the hell out of Chugwater or else," Annie was saying. "He's gone!"

"You sure?" It seemed too good to be true.

"Yep. Hightailed it outa here to North Dakota, the Bakken oil fields. Good riddance to bad rubbish. I cannot stomach that creep!"

"I sure hope he stays away." Sara twirled a lock of her hair around her finger.

"I think he will, sweetie. He knows those guys mean business."

Sara realized how much she missed Chugwater. She loved her little town.

"How's the trip going?"

"I love driving the semi, Annie."

"Good! And Hank the Cowboy?"

"He's great. Amazing."

"Uh oh, I hear something in your voice."

"No, really. He's great."

"But?"

"But, well, seems like he knows all the damned waitresses."

"Oh."

"It's making me crazy."

"Because you care."

"Why the hell can't I just relax and enjoy this?"

"Is something else wrong?"

"No. Just stupid insecurities."

Annie was silent.

"But I'm excited!" Sara chirped. "I mean, I'm driving a friggin' semi, for cryin' out loud!"

"I'm happy for you, girl. I know how long you've been wanting that. I'm gonna miss you, though."

"I'll be in there all the time, bugging you. You can't get rid of me that easily, Annie."

***

"Hand me my hairbrush, would you, Becky?"

Sara blinked, her eyes wide. Sitting on the bed unbuttoning her shirt, she froze. Had she heard him right? She handed him the brush, staring at him.

"What?" He unfastened his ponytail and began brushing his long hair.

"Nothing." She turned away. What the hell, it was probably natural to have a slip of the tongue like that. Maybe she should be surprised it hadn't happened before this.

But it bugged her. Really bugged her. Sara took a deep breath. She needed some air. And some time. Glancing out the sleeper's side window, she decided to take a little walk around the rest area. It was really dark, but so what? She grabbed her new LED flashlight from her bag and pulled her tennis shoes back on.

"I'm going for a walk," she said, trying to sound light, casual.

"Sounds good. I need to stretch my legs."

"Actually, I feel like being alone."

He stopped brushing his hair. "Everything OK?"

"Sure," she lied, fidgeting with her flashlight and wishing she had the guts to level with him about how she felt. "Sometimes I need alone time, that's all."

Hank nodded. "Makes sense, babe. Watch for snakes, OK? Stay on the pavement and use your flashlight."

"OK." Sara swung out the passenger door and clambered down the laddered steps. Snakes, huh? She shuddered, shining her flashlight around the truck. On the Interstate, someone geared down with a loud, whining jake brake. Sara watched the light northbound traffic out there. Maybe she would just leave. It would be easy to hitchhike out of this rest area.

She might just do that. She inhaled the fresh night air and caught the scent of wet dirt. Was a rain shower coming? The other three semis parked here were dark. It was pretty late. Sara leaned against the semi and scanned the clear night sky. It was beautiful out here.

Even though they'd had a relaxing evening of hot springs soaking, she was tense. Something was building in her, something that smelled like fear. Something building like the humidity before a thunderstorm. She had to wonder if she was being truly crazy.

If only Hank would tell her how he felt. Sara was trying to be mellow, but she knew she couldn't continue like this much longer. She kept looking to him for some sense of security in the relationship, even though she knew damned well it was too early for that sort of thing.

She gazed at the Big Dipper. It was up to her to be secure with herself. Dang! She knew the only true source of security is from within herself. But right now she couldn't find her inner security. Maybe she was too scared.

It hurt, hearing him call her Becky. She knew it wasn't his fault, but it felt scary. It triggered something deep inside her, a terrible fear that she wasn't lovable.

She sighed, looking at the stars again. Sauntering over to a picnic table, she sat down. Sara did NOT want to screw this up. This thing with Hank was good.

But maybe she was in over her head. Maybe she couldn't handle this, or him.

Richard's face flashed into her mind. Oh great, she thought, tossing her head as if she could shake away his image. Maybe that was the answer. Maybe her bad marriage to him was fueling her problem now. Was that why Sara couldn't tell Hank how she felt? Was that why she felt threatened by Hank's waitress friends?

She remembered a quote she'd read long ago: "To love at all is to be vulnerable." It had been years since the abuse from Richard, she reminded herself. She believed Hank to be trustworthy. In the long run, trust was absolutely necessary if she wanted love in her life.

And she did want it.

It was a matter or relearning to trust. Maybe she could level with Hank about what had gone on in that marriage, and how it was affecting her now. Yeah, that was what she needed to do. He deserved to know what she'd gone through.

She would think of it as training. That was what the counselor had said. That she should be patient with herself because it might be slow going. Maybe she could find a counselor again. And talk to Annie. Annie was so wise!

She could still hear Richard's hateful voice: "No one will ever care about you."

Why was it so easy to believe that horrible man?

Richard's lies and his verbal abuse had turned out to be more damaging than the physical violence he'd dished out. And he'd dished out plenty of that.

Sara knew she could turn to her friends in Chugwater. She was glad that they'd be home soon. She took deep breaths, studying the stars again.

What was it the counselor had told her? She believed Sara

had PTSD – Post Traumatic Stress Disorder. The counselor had suggested she join a support group in Cheyenne, where she could talk with other abuse survivors. Maybe the time had come to find a group.

She could hear Annie's voice in her ear: "What's the worst that can happen?"

The worst would be failing.

No, the worst would be not to try.

Struggling was human, that was all there was to it. And Sara knew that for her, struggling to trust was a sign of healing.

At that moment a brilliant shooting star streaked down to the horizon.

Sara loved seeing things like that. What was it Mom had always told her? When you see a shooting star, make the best wish you can think of. She leaned back on her hands, smiled, and closed her eyes.

"My wish is to learn to trust again," she whispered. She opened her eyes and basked in the desert starlight.

CHAPTER 27

HANK

He was vaguely uncomfortable with Sara wanting to be alone.

Give her space, he told himself. Everyone needed space sometimes.

But he sensed that something had shifted, that she was pulling back. Hank could feel it in the achy pit of his stomach. He plumped up a pillow and changed the TV channel to The Tonight Show.

His eyes were getting heavy by the time Sara climbed back into the semi.

"I saw the most beautiful shooting star," she said. "I wish you could have seen it."

"Me too. I love falling stars." He glanced at her. Now was as good a time as any, he figured. Just dive in, he told himself. "Sara, what's going on?"

"What do you mean?"

"You're pulling away from me."

She joined him on the bed, sitting up and crossing her legs Indian style. "Yeah, we need to talk."

"Shit," he muttered, "everyone knows what that usually means."

"No…"

"OK."

"I haven't wanted to bring it up. I hate to admit it…"

"What?"

"That it bothers me, how you have so many waitress friends."

"Really?"

"Yes, well, that one, you were talking to her. When I came back from the bathroom you both clammed up. I hate stuff like that! That really made me wonder…"

"Oh." He didn't blame her one bit, but how to tell her about Dixie? And Charlie? His son was such a hot mess.

Sara waited for him to go on, her head cocked to one side.

"I've been meaning to tell you." Hank's mind raced, trying to come up with an excuse for having kept this from Sara.

"Tell me what?" She looked worried.

"Dixie's my ex-girlfriend."

"She is?"

"From long ago."

"You could have told me."

He nodded, wishing to hell he'd told her before now.

"Why didn't you?"

"I don't know," he said, rubbing his jaw. "Well, I do, kind of … it's hard to talk about it."

"Hard to talk about your ex-girlfriend? What happened to us telling each other everything?" Her voice was rising. "Do I get to punish YOU now?"

She was losing her temper. Hank had never heard such a sharp, angry edge in Sara's voice. He frowned. "I think you better calm down."

"CALM DOWN? I'll decide when to fucking calm down!"

"Sara…"

"What?! You say this Dixie's your ex-girlfriend. But I can tell she's interested in you now."

"No way."

Sara stared at him.

"We keep in touch," he said softly.

She raised her eyebrows at him.

"We're friends because of Charlie." Oh boy, she was really going to flip her lid when she heard the next part.

"Charlie?"

"Our son."

"What???" Sara's jaw dropped.

"All of this is ancient history but—"

"I thought I knew you!" She folded her arms across her chest and shifted on the bed, putting more distance between them.

"I went with Dixie years ago. We were barely out of high school and she got pregnant. She decided to marry someone else, but have the baby. Now he's grown up."

"Where is he?"

"Phoenix…"

Her jaw dropped again. "We could have stopped there to see him!"

He scratched the back of his neck. "But, well, the thing is, he's a mess. Drugs."

"Oh."

"Heroin."

"Oh my God."

"It's not something I talk about."

"Understandable, but we agreed to be honest with each other."

"I know." Hank couldn't read the expression on her face. "I'm afraid he'll overdose…"

"That's tough."

He nodded.

"But I really thought we were telling each other everything."

He hung his head, trying to think of something to say to make her feel better.

"I don't see how I can trust you."

"That's everything, I swear."

"This isn't going to work." Sara shook her head. She moved over to the cupboard, took out her duffle bag, and began throwing clothes in it.

"What are you doing?"

"I'm outa here."

"Sara!" This was not happening. Everything seemed to go in slow motion.

"I can't handle this."

"Come on!"

"I knew there was something...I was already thinking of taking off..."

"I know I should have told you."

"I just can't do this, Hank."

He stared at her. "What???" This was not the Sara he knew and loved.

"I'm sorry." Her tone of voice sounded anything but sorry as she ripped through the sleeper cabinets and threw things onto the bed, almost hitting him a couple times.

Hank had no words. Had she lost her ever-loving mind or what?

"I've done lots of hitchhiking. It's not that far."

"I'm not gonna let you hitchhike..."

"LET me?"

Again he stared at her, at a loss for words.

"LET me?" she repeated, hands on her hips and eyes blazing.

"Come on, let's talk this out."

"I won't spend one more minute with you, Hank Werner!" She yanked her waitress skirt from the cabinet and threw it at him. "Here ya go! You can HAVE the stupid goddam skirt, you like it so much!" Sara slammed the cabinet door, hard. "I'm keeping the goddam fucking high heels, though," she muttered, opening another cupboard.

"Sara, please." He took her by the shoulders, trying to stop her.

She shook his hands off. "You're bad for me. I know that now."

"No! We're fantastic together!" Was she really going to do this?

She slammed more doors and yanked the zipper of her duffle bag closed.

"I can't believe this…"

"Well, believe it!" She opened the passenger door, tossed the bag onto the ground, and scrambled down to the pavement.

He couldn't let her do this. Hank clambered down behind her. In the shadowy light coming from his sleeper's windows, he grabbed her arm.

"DON'T TOUCH ME!" she shrieked, her eyes flashing furiously.

Lights came on in two of the other semis that were parked in the rest area. Oh boy, he thought. Here we go. Doors opened. Two women came out. "Need anything, honey?" one said to Sara.

"It's ok," she told them. "Sorry to disturb you."

"No problem," the woman called. "You sure you're all right?"

"Yep, I'm sure. Thanks for the offer!"

"SARA!" he hissed as the women went back in.

"Leave me alone!" she hissed back.

"This is me!" He slammed his chest with both of his hands. "Don't you care enough to give me the benefit of the doubt?"

She turned toward him and paused. "You know I care," she said slowly.

"So do I…"

"Do you?" she asked, so faintly he barely heard her.

"You know I do!"

See, that's the thing. I don't know that."

"What?"

"I don't know how you feel. You never say anything … and I care too much."

"But—"

"But what?" She had her hands on her hips again.

"What do you mean you care too much?" He watched her closely, the sharp angles of her cheekbones catching the dim light from the side window of the sleeper.

"It's just me…"

He could hear the struggle in her voice. Sara was trying hard to control herself. She was trying to avoid a massive outburst. "Go on," he said gently.

"I always care too much."

Hank stood there looking at her, too confused to speak. He felt dumb. He didn't really understand what she was saying. She always cared too much? What did that mean? But he had to do something, say something. He couldn't let her leave. "I LOVE YOU, SARA COOKE!" his mind screamed at her.

But the words were stuck in his throat.

He simply could not say them.

"Why didn't you tell me about Charlie, and Dixie?" she was asking.

He wagged his head and threw his hands up to the sky. "I don't know."

She began to turn away.

"Because I'm a goddam dumbshit!" Hank blurted.

Sara stopped, turned back, and put her bag down on the pavement. Again she folded her arms across her chest. "Well, that's true enough."

He couldn't tell if she was smirking at him. So what if she was? He just had to get her to listen. "I've never told anyone about Charlie. I was afraid of what you would think, Sara. Now I've made it worse…"

"Yes, you have."

He caressed her cheek. "Give me another chance?"

She was silent, her eyes searching his as he cupped her delicate jaw in his hand.

He moved in and gave her a deep kiss.

She let him kiss her a little. Then she pulled back.

"What we have is wonderful, Sara."

"I know," she whispered, "but it scares me..." Those wide eyes of hers flicked up to his but darted away again.

"It scares me too!" Hank murmured.

"It does?" Sara looked surprised.

"Of course!" How could she not know it scared him too, he wondered. Maybe she was right. Maybe he hadn't been communicating openly.

"Another chance, huh?"

"Yep." He held his breath and prayed that she'd stay.

Sara quickly swung her bag around, as if to smack him with it. "Don't blow it, Bucko!"

He grabbed the duffle bag and used it to lead her back to the semi. Thank God! He would make this right. Hoisting her bag into the cab, Hank waited for Sara to climb in, then followed her.

She perched on the passenger seat, swiveling around to face the bed.

He sat on the bed and reached over to get them each a beer from the fridge.

Her eyes glued to his, she opened her beer and took a hefty swig. And waited.

"All right, here's the deal," Hank said. "Becky was my only love. There has never been anyone else, until you."

"You swear you're being honest with me?"

"Yes I do. I'm being totally honest!"

"OK."

"The thing is, it's impossible to get over Becky..."

Again Sara waited.

"...even though she would want me to get on with my life."

She nodded.

"I've been stuck for years."

"Me too," Sara whispered.

"Then you…"

She seemed to hold her breath, her eyes shining in the dim light.

"…You blew me apart!"

"What?" Again she looked surprised.

Now or never, he told himself. Time to take the plunge and to hell with it. "I love you, Sara!" The words burst from his lips like a fireworks explosion. Hank felt his cheeks burning.

Sara's wide smile lit up her face like sunshine emerging from a big, dark cloud. She jumped up and wrapped her arms around his neck. "And I love you, Hank!"

"You do?"

"YES!"

Their lips met in a fiery kiss. They took each other's mouths with a passion inspired by jeopardy. They'd come so close to losing each other.

Hank pulled her onto his lap, held her tight, and kissed her harder. He felt like he was back in high school, making out like this. This time it was all about the emotions. For once he didn't think about taking it further.

Sara's lips lingered on his, deepening their kiss as she moaned a little.

His tongue explored hers.

She explored him right back.

"Mmmm," he groaned, finally coming up for air. "I don't want to ever lose you, Sara."

"I don't want to lose you either, Hank Werner!"

His lips slid down to the side of her neck.

"Let's be careful with each other," she whispered.

"Yes," he said into her neck. "No more secrets."

"Absolutely," she agreed breathlessly.

His lips moved to her collar bone. "I had no idea you were

feeling insecure."

Sara stroked his hair. "I do hide things like that pretty well."

He nodded.

"Trust is really hard for me, Hank."

He lifted his head and looked into her eyes. "And talking is tough for me."

She nodded. "It takes a lot to build my trust…"

He held her hand, stroking the back of it with his thumb.

"…then if it's broken, I'm famous for never giving it back."

"You can trust me," he told her.

"I get that here," she said, pointing to her head. "But I don't get it here." She put her other hand over her heart.

"I want you to trust me."

"And I want to trust you."

He nodded. "Richard?"

"That's part of it."

"Only part of it, huh?"

"Right. It goes way back…"

He waited.

"The only reason I stayed with someone like Richard was because of how I grew up."

"I get that."

"You do?"

"Oh yes." Hank nuzzled her neck with his nose.

"We both have long stories, I'm sure."

"Yep."

"I'd love to hear yours, Hank."

"And I'd love to hear yours," he murmured, kissing her collar bone again. "But not now, ok?"

Sara chuckled softly. "OK," she agreed, ruffling his hair with her fingers. "But soon?"

"Yep." He slid his hands under her shirt. Her skin was warm and silky.

"One more thing?"

He groaned.

Sara took his face in her hands and gazed straight into his eyes. "Let's promise that even if we're scared, we'll be honest and open with each other."

She was right, of course. Honesty was key. "All right," he said. "I promise."

"I promise, too," she whispered.

Hank lay her on the bed, stretched out next to her, and took her mouth again.

She opened to him, heat radiating from her.

His lips explored her breasts, making her sigh and arch up. He loved it when she did that. He kissed her belly, moving his lips down to her navel.

"Ooh," she whimpered, her fingernails digging lightly into his shoulders.

This was a night for savoring. A night for relishing every sound, every sight, every touch, every taste of her.

CHAPTER 28

SARA

She sat on the bed behind the curtain, pulling on her strappy high heels. Sara felt the semi pulling a long grade. They were almost to the Wyoming line. She fastened the tiny buckles, stood, and smoothed down the new red mini-skirt she'd bought to surprise Hank. He would go crazy when he saw this red skirt.

She opened the curtain and tied back the panels.

Hank glanced over. "My, my."

Sara sauntered over to the passenger seat, showing off the new skirt. She sank into the seat and crossed her legs, wiggling one high-heel-clad foot in the air.

"Nice," he said.

"Why, thank you, Hank."

"Not as nice as your waitress skirt, though."

Her mouth flew open in surprise. "You've GOT to be kidding!"

"I am." He winked at her.

She shook her head, trying not to blush.

"Time for your next lesson." He patted the top of his right thigh.

Sara ducked under his arm and slid onto his lap.

"Steer." Hank kept his foot on the accelerator pedal.

She took the wheel, shivering as he ran his fingernails up her bare arms.

Hank kissed the side of her neck and slowly moved his mouth up to her ear. Kissing her behind her ear, he caressed her other ear lobe.

Sara melted, trying to concentrate on keeping the semi between the lane lines. She kept thinking things would calm down between her and Hank. But he just got sexier and sexier.

He kissed her jawline and ran his big hands up and down her arms again.

She felt her nipples go hard as he lightly brushed them with the back of his hand. Sara loved his touch so much, she felt she might swoon.

He kissed her behind the ear again, moving his mouth down her neck. Slowly unbuttoning her white blouse, Hank pushed it off her shoulders and kissed her there, too. He ran his hands lightly down her thighs and stroked the skin behind her knees.

Sara moaned softly. She was glad the traffic was light on the interstate today. They had this stretch of road pretty much to themselves. "Let's pull over," she said.

"No." He kissed her neck again.

Sara adored the steamy heat of his breath on her skin.

"You taste good, babe." He unhurriedly stroked her knees.

If only she could just pull over. She gasped as his fingernails lightly tickled the backs of her knees.

Hank stroked one of her calves. He took off her sparkly high heel and rubbed her arch with his thumb.

"Ohhhh," she sighed.

He rubbed her toes, pushing his big fingers between her toes.

Wow, that was incredibly sexy. Sara wanted to memorize this feeling, this moment. His touch was so loving and so erotic. As his fingers rubbed the delicate skin between her toes, her center dissolved into a white-hot flow of molten lava.

Hank stroked her other calf, took off her other shoe, and massaged that foot. He caressed her hair and massaged her scalp with sweeping strokes as he nibbled on the back of her neck. "You are one sexy woman, partner."

"Partner?" Sara wanted to turn around and look at him, but had to watch the road, dammit.

"Yep. Partner."

"As in trucking partner?"

"Yep."

"Really?" This was huge.

"Sara..."

"Yes..."

"I love you." His voice was deep as he said it.

"I love you, Hank." She meant it with every fiber of her being.

"Be my wife."

"What?"

"You heard me."

Sara held her breath, her mind racing. A marriage proposal? Now? Was he trying to make her crash them into a ditch? Here she was on his lap, hands clenched as she steered the rig, Hank holding one of her bare feet and stroking her hair. Then again, maybe this was the perfect place and time for a marriage proposal from a man like Hank. A sexy man who knew what he wanted and was not afraid to take it. A sensual man who made her happy – on every level.

"Well?" he was asking.

"Yes!" She exhaled with a whoosh.

"Mmmmm, good," he murmured into her hair, his hands moving to her thighs. He played with the hem of her skirt, pushing it up.

Sara tried to swat his hands away.

"Hands on the wheel," Hank growled.

** The End **

ABOUT THE AUTHOR

Margaret Harlowe
is an award-winning author
of naughty erotic romance.
She enjoys her wicked imagination,
and
hopes you do, too.

Find her on Twitter: @authormharlowe

Made in the USA
Charleston, SC
03 September 2016